Hopeless Sacrifice

Hopeless Sacrifice

A.K. Koonce

*To the Hopeless. May they survive the ash and dust
and live to rise again.*

Table of Contents

Chapter One
The Gods Above

The Realm of the Gods is as captivating as I always imagined it would be. We stare up at the entrance from our meager little existence. Thousands of stairs tower up, taunting us to journey forward. I take the first step, and Ryder, Darrio, and Daxdyn hold their gaze on me even after I pass them. Nefarious gives a little smoky exhale as if he's reluctant to follow after me. But he does. His hooves beat hard against the granite.

The hollow echo of my boots against the ancient stone fills the air until one after the other they trail behind me. The repetitive sound of the soldiers' steps consumes my mind. It's a nice, steady beat. Strands of my long blonde hair blow across my face on the cool breeze as I trek higher into the heavens.

The gods are really just above here? Do they know we're coming? Do they know what our futures hold?

It's an endless and quiet hike. An hour passes in heavy silence. It's as if everyone else is thinking the same stream of anxious thoughts that I am.

1

When the air thins out with a drifting layer of fog guiding our steps, I see it. A shining, golden gate is just ahead. My steps become faster, tapping quickly against the stone.

The gates part upon my arrival, gliding open and letting the heavens greet me as if they've been waiting for me my entire life.

Soft ground meets my feet, the fog thickening around my calves.

A long white desk sits in the middle of an open and empty space. Everything is white and hazy. It feels like my mind's playing tricks on me, not letting me fully see what's around us. I blink rapidly to clear my gaze but nothing helps.

Daxdyn's warm hand slips into mine, his lips skimming the corner of my jaw as he leans into my body.

"The gods aren't ... as honest and helpful as you might think." I peek up at his serious look. "Be careful with your requests." His lips press to my temple before he pulls away.

I should be careful? They are the ones who said this would be the best route back to the mortal realm.

"Next," a woman shrieks to no one in particular.

My spine stiffens from her tone and I stand on the

toes of my boots to see a small woman seated behind the enormous desk.

"Next," she beckons again.

I hesitantly walk forward. Darrio's arm skims mine as he keeps a protective pace with me.

Hundreds of soldiers stand quietly behind us as I step up to the desk.

My fingers run over the smooth surface. I look down at her. Glossy brown hair is tied tightly back from her porcelain features. She's young. Pretty. Beautiful really.

Seconds pass as I wait for her to tip her head up at me. To acknowledge me in some way. Still, she just sorts through her stack of papers, signing her name at the bottom of some and shuffling others into a separate bin on her desk.

It's all very mundane.

Not very godly at all.

"Can I help you?" Her eyes never leave the documents in front of her. For a moment, I look up at Darrio. He passes me a stern but annoyed look.

"Yes, I—we'd like to speak to someone within the Realm of the Gods. There's a war c—"

Her bland tone cuts me off before I can even

consider my words fully.

"Do you have an appointment?"

A line creases her thin brows. A beat passes with the scratching sound of her pen as she signs off on another paper.

An appointment? Do I look like the type of person who has their shit together enough for appointments?

"Um, no. No, we don't, but it is a matter of importance."

Desperately, I cling to the most professional persona I can.

A matter of importance. Who the hell says stuff like that?

"Unfortunately, no one is granted access within the Realm of the Gods unless they have been summoned." Her blue eyes look up at me for less than a second, judging me entirely within that short amount of time.

Dread sinks heavy to the bottom of my stomach.

Of course. Why would we be allowed to just prance into the Realm of the Gods?

"I've been summoned," Ryder says, stepping forward, his fingers drumming against the shining desktop as he offers her a charming smile.

I keep the skeptical look from my face as he leans into her little area.

"Viola summoned me this morning. *Again.*" He winks at her, and I nearly give myself an aneurism to keep from rolling my eyes at his ridiculous charisma.

"Viola?" The paper is set down as she looks up at the former prince of Juvar. "Have you brought your heritage documentation?" Her eyes narrow on him, disbelief lacing her words.

"Of course." Ryder pulls a folded paper from his pocket but doesn't hand it to her. It's a piece of trash for sure, but it is a neatly folded piece of trash.

"I'll need three legal proofs of residency as well." Her voice is a testing sound, seemingly waiting for him to back down from her requests.

Proofs of residency? Well I'm screwed.

Guess the fate of the mortal realm is on Ryder's arrogant shoulders now.

"Of course." Ryder's smile widens as if this is a typical day filled with typical paperwork. Just another day within the Realm of the Gods for dear old Ryder. "Can you give her a call? She's going to be upset if I'm late this time."

The woman studies Ryder. She seems to be

5

considering him very intently. I look away, feigning interest in the emptiness that surrounds me.

After she's looked at the handsome prince for all he's worth, she slowly picks up a small, white, square object. Her polished red nails press a few buttons on the thing before she holds it between her shoulder and her ear.

Her pen scrawls across another document as she signs it quickly.

"Viola, good morning." The sweetest tone I've ever heard falls from her lips as a false smile perches against her mouth. "I have a man here," she pauses and glances up at Ryder.

"Ryder Rourke," he whispers, leaning even closer to her, charm rolling off of him in suffocating waves.

"Ryder Rourke says you summoned him again." Her gaze shifts skeptically over Ryder's wide shoulders. "Yes, he is. He's brought a few … friends this time." Her attention flickers to me and the crowd of soldiers. "Yes. I'll let him know. Thank you."

A button is pressed against the tiny box before she sets it down.

My heart pounds, waiting for her to speak again.

"Viola will be right out, Mr. Rourke."

Fuck yes!

Ryder passes me a confident look from out of the corner of his eye and it has energy searing through me. I almost throw my arms around him. The woman's annoyance and glaring eyes hold me in my place. But it doesn't stop the smile of achievement from consuming my features.

The four of us drift away from her desk, just to put a safe amount of space between us and her. The soldiers stand quiet; a mass of trained precision and deadly strength. Darrio steps away from us and whispers something quietly to his second in command.

Unfortunately, the second in command, Streven, reminds me just how little faith he has in me as he holds my gaze. His sea blue eyes sink into me as Darrio speaks in a low, humming tone to him.

My attention trails over the others. A look of respect passes my way, some of them lower their gazes entirely. None hold the doubt that Streven does.

Not that I'm dwelling on it. Not everyone will love my endearing and fabulous fucking personality.

I turn away from him, and Ryder's wide chest skims my arm.

"Who's Viola?" I whisper, tipping my head up to him in hopes that my voice doesn't carry to the hard-glaring receptionist.

Ryder's mouth parts but he doesn't immediately answer. The warmth of his palm skims down the inside of my wrist, just across the dark lines of the Hopeless symbol, as his body dominates over mine. He seems to be thinking through his words carefully.

"Yes, who *is* Viola, Ryder?" Daxdyn taunts him with a mischievous smile that even the gods would be envious of.

At the tone of his voice my eyes narrow, my head tilting back to consider the silence Ryder's clinging to.

"Well," another long pause cuts through his words.

As I stare up at him, my chest pressing against his, his breath fanning over my lips, a woman appears from thin air. Her features blur before turning into a solid form.

My steps falter away from her, stumbling against the pure white fog.

"*I* am Viola." White teeth reveal a wide and astoundingly beautiful smile. Emerald eyes shine down on me. Every single inch of her is smooth perfection.

Her gaze dances between Ryder and myself, her attention finally settling curiously on the prince.

"Ryder, how are you?" The spark in her eyes shifts

all over his body, skimming against his muscle tone and the uneasy look in his eyes.

You know that tension that fires through a room when two people who have had sex meet again? That tension is blazing this fucking realm to the ground.

She's enjoying the teetering awkwardness Ryder's trying to hide. She looks like a hungry cat toying with the carcass of a mouse.

"Who's your friend, Ryder?" The smile on her lips grows.

His palm pushes down my hand, his fingers interlocking with mine.

"This is Zakara Storm." A gentle pause has me hanging on his words. "My girlfriend." A weird feeling floods my heart. It consumes me with a strange and unexpected happiness. "Kara, this is Viola, keeper of the past, seer of the realms, speaker of the gods."

Fucker of my boyfriend.

The pettiness is pushed down deep inside me as I offer her a kind smile.

Is there a realm somewhere—anywhere—that isn't filled with women Ryder has screwed?

My annoyed thoughts are cut off when she asks the real question that's needed here.

"I haven't seen you in a while. What do you need now, fae?" A teasing smirk fills her pretty features and she begins to look around at the endless army behind me.

"A violent war is coming to the mortal realm and soon to ours." Ryder's deep tone vibrates through the empty space in a strange way.

"Yes. Yes, it is." Her voice is soft and calm.

The aloof sound of her words, the carelessness of it, sets me on edge.

We're talking about the annihilation of an entire realm and this keeper-speaker can't seem to focus on a thing we're saying.

"We want the gods' help," I blurt out, tilting my head into her view, drawing her attention back to the very real issue at hand.

The curious look in her eyes dances over my features, taking in every detail of my face.

"No." A playful smile accompanies her reply.

"No?"

"The gods do not intervene with petty mortal problems."

Petty?

Petty?

She wants to see petty?

Daxdyn's palm skims down my spine, his magic threatening to smother out the outrage that's building within me.

"Can we just come in and discuss this, Vi?" A smile that makes me want to slap him fills Ryder's face.

Vi?

Childish aggravation swarms me.

"I cannot entertain an entire army, Ryder. I *do* want to know more about her though." Her gaze settles back on the line that's creasing hard through my brows. "I want to know why the gods chose her above all others."

You and me both, Vi.

"Come, bring your lovers as well." The knowing look in her gaze skips between Darrio, Daxdyn, and Ryder.

Only a short second passes before she turns to leave. The four of us trail behind the pretty goddess. The secretary gives us a quick look from over her tower of papers as we pass. It takes everything in me not to flip her off.

The fog clears away the farther into the realm we journey. Colors begin to push into view, deep shades of

11

green and blues. A land similar to the Hopeless realm materializes as if it has surrounded us the whole time and we just now have the ability to see it.

Lush grass guides me forward. The sky is a perfect shade of blue and trees bloom with pale pink flowers. The smell of nature envelops me. Pools of crystal-clear water skim against the edge of our path as I trail after the swaying steps of the goddess.

A courtyard makes way to an open setting and it's there that we stop. Few people–gods—linger in the area. They speak quietly, ignoring the five of us.

Except for one.

Deep blue eyes continue to lock on to mine, following me as I walk behind Viola. The hulking man looks out of place among the serene flowers.

I suppose we do too.

We only make it a few yards in before he wanders slowly over. His chest is bare, revealing the perfectly sculpted body only a god could have.

"I didn't know we had visitors today." Confidence clings to his deep voice as he looks to Viola for an introduction.

A catlike smile is all she gives him. No introductions. Nothing. She gives the god nothing.

Maybe I do like her after all.

"I'm Baldur. Welcome to the realm." Baldur's hand is extended to me and the fact that his warm attention is held solely on me does not go unnoticed.

Stiffly, I take his hand. I shake it with cautionary instincts slashing through my chest. Everything here is beautiful and perfect and accompanied by a feeling of unease.

"Baldur, do not bore our new guests already." An airy tone drifts through a new stranger's words as he clasps Baldur on the shoulder, standing too close it seems. Baldur's shoulder's tense beneath the man's touch.

"You four want something, yes?" The newcomer's pale eyes crinkle at the corners.

"Yes," I say without hesitation.

The stranger's gaze flashes, a bright white flickering through the blue.

"I'm Loki. Please, please tell me what the gods can do for you."

It's then that the rug is pulled out. Loki is not one to ask favors of. In fact, I'd like to step back from him entirely.

Darrio takes a single step closer to me and Loki's

wild eyes eat up the small movement.

"You two are … a temporary item."

Temporary?

"Passing love is always the best." A romantic sigh leaves his lips as he looks off into the sky with a deranged smile.

"Actually, all four of them are an item." Viola and Loki share a similar manic look.

Is everyone here fucking insane?

Loki's hungry gaze shifts over us, his attention lingers longer on Ryder and Dax.

"The blonde man and the smaller man do seem to be a perfect match."

Ryder's eyes widen as if he's just been struck down by the wrath of the gods.

"That's … not …" Daxdyn's argument fades away as he struggles to explain the four of us.

"They're in love with the woman, Loki." Viola explains and another curious look slashes white through his gaze. Baldur still hasn't looked away from me, and I keep my shoulders locked in an image of strength.

"She has fire magic. She has wings too." Viola's voice holds so much wonder in it that I'm starting to feel like

Chapter Two

Puppet Fucking

Viola leads us to a palace. Its peaks are impossibly high, reaching up into the already thinning heavens. We trek through twisting staircases. Nightfall kisses the horizon as we climb to the top floor.

Loki promised me we'd settle this tomorrow with a bigger *audience*. The way he said audience still lingers in my thoughts.

"Vi, we can't stay here. Our realms are in danger, our soldiers are waiting for us. We cannot waste time here." A tired and worn sound fills Ryder's voice. We stand in a dark hall in front of a door. Gold lines swirl across the wooden door. The details sway over the surface, catching the light before drifting farther with shimmering magic.

"Time does not exist for the gods. Each day passes at our own pace. You've been here for what seems like hours, but in your realm only a few minutes have passed." Viola's gaze dances across Ryder's perfect features. She seems to be memorizing them or remembering them.

17

"The time you spend here with us will never be a waste." It's said in a whisper; a sad tone that fades away as she steps past us, walking quickly back the way we just came.

The four of us stand quietly alone as her footsteps echo through the castle.

Hesitantly, I turn the gold knob and push open the door. Upon opening, a soft golden light warms the room. It tingles across my flesh. The source of the light is unseen. It simply … exists.

An echo sounds through the room with every step I take. The cobble floors are spotless and lead to a grand space that I wasn't expecting. The widest bed I've ever seen sits on the far wall. A comforter of deep mossy green is snugly pressed over the mattress. Gold trim highlights the ceilings, making every angle of it shine in the warm lighting. A deep bath similar to a pool takes up the far corner, and clear water drifts through it invitingly.

A single window takes up the opposite wall, looking out into the crystal white stars of the night sky. The heavens look pure and bright from here. Seconds pass and still I just stand in the center of the room, staring out at the intensity of the moon.

"What do you think Loki's planning?" Dax asks. He leans against the edge of the bed, crossing one ankle over the other before folding his arms. He looks careless and confident.

Ryder sits on the edge of the bath, his fingers gliding through the surface of the water. His attention is held on the depths of it.

"Nothing good." Ryder's vague comment sounds distracted, filled with thought.

My brows pull together as I try to think about what Loki could possibly want in exchange for his help. Why didn't Baldur offer his help? If they aren't to get involved in mortal issues, perhaps Loki has no intention of helping us at all. Darrio steps closer to me, his palm skimming down my ribs, making me shiver against his touch.

"We're going to be ready for it whatever it is." The promising sound of Darrio's tone makes some of the tension fall away.

The other two men look at me, and suddenly I realize my worry is making them worry more.

Shit.

"Come take a bath with me." Darrio's tone is gentle and quiet and throws me so far off guard that I physically stumble back to look at him.

He … wants to take a bath with me … with two other

19

men?

It's just a bath. Why am I being so emotional over a bath? I need to pull my shit together or these men will think I'm as breakable as they always try to treat me. I can't help it, my heart melts because he's trying. He's trying so hard to make me happy, and I love him completely for it.

"Okay." It's the shyest my voice has ever sounded in my entire life.

Ryder and Daxdyn seem equally unsure of themselves as Darrio takes my hand and leads me to the bath. Ryder even steps aside for us. The prince's hands shove into his pockets as he stands with the most unsure look on his face.

Daxdyn doesn't seem to have a shitty comment for his brother for once. Everyone is a chain of support in this moment; supporting Darrio to support me.

Why does that make me want to cry? When did these assholes have to turn into the sweetest men I know? It was so much easier when they were just self-centered jerks. I can't believe I actually prefer it when they're total assholes. At least then I know what to expect.

I swallow down the rising emotions. Darrio's fingers push up my abdomen slowly and lightly. The white shirt raises against his palm and I arch into his touch. His stormy eyes hold mine as he pushes the material up my chest. I raise my arms for him as he pulls it off. Silence like I've never heard before clings to the room.

With care, he unfastens my jeans. Big hands skim across my outer thighs as he pushes my jeans and underwear down. I try my best not to melt into his touch. His strong shoulders meet my palms. I lean against him and kick off my boots and clothes.

And then I'm naked.

I'm naked before the three men I love. My attention drifts to Ryder. The intensity of his pale gaze skims across my chest. Does he know I love him?

My heart thunders hard and strong.

I love him?

It isn't something I've confessed to even myself yet.

Darrio steps back from me. His hand grips the back of his shirt as he begins pulling slowly. A mixture of hard muscle and soft scars line his abdomen.

If he feels awkward in front of the other two men, he doesn't show it. I suppose he's been naked in front of other men before. He's two hundred years old and a commander of the largest army in the seven realms.

It's not like he has anything to be ashamed about.

His jeans shove to the floor with a quiet clicking sound of his belt hitting cement. My eyes wander down the veering lines of his hips and I'm reminded just how *very* much he shouldn't be ashamed.

Once again, he takes my hand. His long legs step over the ledge and slosh into the water. Warm droplets of it hit my stomach and slide down my skin. With both hands, Darrio helps me step into the bath. His palms grip my hips, pulling me toward him. The water skims across my breasts before stopping just below my shoulders.

It isn't hot, but it is relaxing. The feel of his hands slick on my body is relaxing and energizing all at once. When my chest brushes against his, the long, hard length of his dick pushes across my inner thigh, making me lean even closer to him.

The golden glow of the lights flickers strangely. I feel the warmth of it drift across my skin with a chill.

His chest brushes against mine. My nipples tighten and I feel the sensation all through my core. Darrio's big palms push down, low against my back, melding my body to his.

"So ... like, can we join you guys or what?" Daxdyn's voice is full of uncertainty. Not a hint of amusement. Just honest confusion about his place in life right now.

My palm settles against Darrio's pounding heart as I

look back at Daxdyn. His leg bounces slightly as his boot taps quickly against the floor. Is he anxious? Nervous? All of the above?

I swim the short space to the edge of the bath. My arms rest against the slick rock and I intentionally pull myself higher, until water glides down the valley between my breasts.

"Only if you want to," I say in a soft voice filled with innocence.

Ryder's gaze follows the water trailing between my breasts and he's moving before the words are fully out of my mouth.

With haste, he pulls off the white shirt, revealing hard lines veering into his tight jeans. Ryder's jeans hit the floor before Dax is even moving. The water is smooth against my skin as I drift back to make room for Ryder. He sits on the edge of the bath before lowering himself slowly down.

The clear waters show me every hard inch of him and it makes my thighs shift together.

Daxdyn takes his time. He's beautiful and he knows he is. He pulls at the shirt. Cut lines of muscle highlight his body in soft shadows against his abdomen and even his sides. Lean muscle covers his body in a lithe form of strength. The odd golden hue of the room gives him a glowing appearance.

I swallow hard, not realizing how truly perfect he is until now.

As he steps over the ledge, I reach out to him, inviting him in.

And he takes the invitation fully. He drifts toward me, wrapping me against his hard body the moment our hands touch. The slick feel of his cock against my thigh makes me grind against him and his lips are on mine in a matter of seconds. He leads me through the water, pushing me back until I'm arching against Darrio's thick length.

I moan against his tongue as he rolls it expertly against mine. Darrio's palms push down my ribs, sending tingles all through my body before locking on to my hips.

Strength surrounds me and I turn slightly, breaking the kiss to reach out to Ryder.

He swims closer, his fingers tangling with mine beneath the water. How does this even work with the four of us? It sounds both exciting and exhausting. They better be prepared to carry me to bed after this.

It's a lot of work taking care of three men. A lot of very, very rewarding work. The benefits are very obvious. Long hours though.

My hand slips away from his. When my fingers wrap around Ryder's cock his eyes flash with a lust filled look. Darrio rolls his hips against the curve of my ass. Daxdyn presses his lips to the base of my neck as he slides the head of his dick against my clit.

Ryder drifts closer as my wrist rolls, my palm taking the length of him. His lashes lower and he presses his lips slowly against mine. Darrio's hand skims up my ribs and his fingers slide across my nipples.

We're a tangled mess of slow and teasing movements. I'm panting against Ryder's mouth and no one's even fucked me yet.

Once more the lighting intensifies a little brighter.

And then a thought has me pulling away from all three of them. I stagger in the waters, sloshing it over the ledge as I struggle to remove myself from between their hard and fantastic bodies. The cold wall meets my back and I look around the room with caution. My gaze trails up to the warm mysterious light.

"Are you okay?" Ryder asks, clearing his throat gruffly.

"Did we hurt you?" Daxdyn reaches out to me.

Darrio steps closer but doesn't touch me.

Their dicks are like compasses pointing true north

I'm the fucking true north here.

Never in my life have I been surrounded by so much dick. And never in my life did I think I'd be complaining about it.

"What if," my voice drops to a conspiratorial whisper, "what if the gods can see us?"

Daxdyn's laugher shakes through his damp chest.

"Then they're some lucky bastards." His laughter quiets to a serious tone. "I imagine some of them probably can." His fingers push through his disorderly hair.

"And that doesn't bother you? That they might be getting off watching us?" My nose scrunches just thinking about it.

"If they can see us here, they could see us in the Hopeless Realm and you weren't too worried about who could see you with Dax and I." Ryder's hands settle on his hips, a confident smirk pulls at his lips.

My thighs shift just thinking about the night I spent with the two of them.

"This is different," I hiss. "The giant bed, the alluring bath, the mood lighting. That doesn't seem … pervy to you?"

Darrio's spine stiffens and he too begins to look up

at the mysterious lighting of the room.

"She's right, this is weird. Like we're puppets they're wanting to watch fuck."

"Puppet fucking? Is that a *thing* for you? A new fetish you forgot to share with us?" Daxdyn cocks a brow at his brother. Darrio settles him with a look of annoyance.

"And with that, I'm done. Apparently, puppet fucking is where I lose my libido at." Ryder climbs from the bath, the water cascading down the panes of his back as he strides away. Roughly he pulls at his jeans, tugging them on and flopping down on the bed without another word.

Daxdyn looks like a puppy that's been kicked too many times in his life. His lips part as he stares across the water at me. The clear bath reflects in his gaze, washing out the color and happiness there. My fingers skim through the waters and I drift closer to him. A chaste kiss is all I give him and he leans into it.

"We need to be rested for whatever tomorrow has in store for us anyway," I whisper.

"You're right. I know you're right."

Deep down my chest aches to be closer to him, wanting to wrap myself up in his warmth instead of dwelling on what tomorrow will bring.

Is he worrying over it too?

"What's wrong?" My finger's tangle through his damp hair as his palms run down my spine before settling low on my back.

"I just want to keep you safe. I wish I could keep you here forever." A smile breaks through his voice but it holds sadness that I can feel shaking through me.

This man would protect me with his last breath. They all would.

Even if I don't need them to.

"I'm not breakable, Dax. I'm … the least breakable person in this room right now."

The word immortal burns through my memory. Mesa was so certain but she wasn't an expert. I'm still not sure how much I believe in my immortality.

Daxdyn's gaze drifts across the features of my face. I feel like he's searching inside me, looking for something that not even I can see.

"You're right." Again, that false smile fills his face, making my heart crumble to little tattered pieces.

"I love you," I whisper it low before pressing my lips against his.

"I love you too." His words catch between our lips

as he flicks his tongue against mine. He kisses me slowly but passionately, dumping all his swirling emotions right into me.

I pull back from him just enough to lean my temple against his, letting droplets from his hair fall into mine.

"Come to bed." My gaze searches his. The pink of his tongue slips between his lips as he nods to me.

The waters shift when I turn to look back at Darrio. He's bathed. While Dax and I had a little heart felt moment, Darrio's washed his hair and body as if we weren't bothering him at all.

The long locks of his hair glisten in the light. His hair isn't normally down and loose. For the most part, it's usually pulled back. It hangs to his shoulders and my fingers twitch to touch it.

"Come to bed," I whisper again and the small sound of my voice commands him. The waters push against Darrio's hard chest as he stalks toward me. His heated gaze burns across my flesh and his attention drifts down to my pebbled nipples.

I shift in Daxdyn's arms.

Darrio slips his fingers through mine and the two men help me from the bath as if I'm a goddess in need of pampering.

Ryder's asleep on top of the soft comforter. He's curled up on his side, taking as little space as possible at the edge. On my hands and knees, I crawl across the monstrosity of a bed until I'm at his side. The cool blankets skim across my calves as I shimmy beneath them. The moment my body aligns against his, he rolls toward me, wrapping his big arm around my small waist. Warm breaths fan across my neck as he hides his face in my hair. Content and exhausted sleep consume the prince of Juvar.

I've exhausted him. I bet his life was simple before we met.

That's a lie, because he was a prisoner when we first met.

Yes, my presence has really changed his life for the better.

It's obvious as we prepare for sleep in the Realm of the Gods, while waiting for a trap set by Loki, before going to war with the great and powerful Eminence.

Changed for the better, I tell you.

Chapter Three

Peace

The cheerful sound of birds and the lustful sound of a groan wakes me the following morning. Darrio's palm splays across my stomach as his hips roll restlessly against my ass. My bare thighs shift smoothly together.

The golden lighting has faded away, replaced by the natural, pale morning sunlight. It strikes through the room in watercolors of blue and white as if the sun has not fully risen.

Unlike the cock pressed low against me.

Ryder sleeps curled up once again. His wide back is to me as I peer around the room. I listen intently but only the birds seem to be awake and ready for the day.

Discreetly, I reach behind me and push my palm over the bulge in Darrio's tight jeans. A shaking breath fans against my neck, making me meld into him even more.

His palm skims slowly down my abdomen. Beneath the blankets, in silence, we explore one another. Touching as if it's the first time.

31

In a way it is.

Everything between Darrio and I has always been so rushed. Hurried and exhilarating, but not caring and caressing.

Not like it is right now.

His fingers push down my sex, dipping low before swirling back to my clit. My eyes clench closed as I try hard not to make a sound.

Once again, I'm having quiet and secretive sex with the asshole fae who stole my heart from the very start.

Soft lips press to the curve of my neck. He takes his time rolling his tongue along my throat before nipping lightly. The rough feel of his beard sends a frenzied feeling right through me.

From behind me, my fingers skim the trail of hair leading down the front of his jeans. The smooth head of his dick rubs over my palm before I wrap my fingers slowly around his length.

His heavy breath is silenced against my neck, rumbling through me with a humming sound of his pleasure.

I only manage to stroke my palm down his cock a few times before he speaks.

"Spread your legs for me." It's a rasping whisper,

spoken as a command and I waste no time doing as I'm told.

The bed dips just slightly as he pushes his jeans down. I'm slick against his tip. The feel of it spirals a reckless energy through my core. Deliberate slowness guides his pace as he sinks in inch by inch. His teeth bite hard against my shoulder to quiet a low growl that shakes through his chest.

With long but leisure strokes, he rocks into me. I arch and shift and grind down the length of his dick until the feeling in my core feels like it's going to combust.

As if time truly does not exist, we spend nearly an hour like that.

He rolls his finger down my folds before rubbing firmly against my clit and the slick feel of him has me coming hard. So hard I cry out just before he pushes his other hand across my mouth. He doesn't cover my cries but instead, his fingers push roughly against my lips, sliding down my jaw. His fingers flex against my throat before tailing across my breast and holding me tightly against him. Harder he thrusts into me, filling me with every inch of him. Stiffly he jerks again once more.

Pulses shake through me from his release as well as my own.

His head settles against my shoulder, his warm

breath fanning down my damp back.

For a few moments, we lie like that. Him still filling me completely while I relax against his chest. The sound of my heart is the only thing I hear for several minutes.

"You know, I really did want to have sex with you with them." It's a quiet confession that has me shifting until he slips from me.

The sheets tangle as I turn to face him.

A sated look is in his beautiful eyes.

I consider his words. His awkward phrasing. He wanted to *have sex with me with them*. Not with us.

A smile pulls at my lips.

"Why?" My tone is quiet but curious.

Ryder shifts, his back meeting mine. From over my shoulder, I look at him to find his face buried beneath a pillow as if someone was disrupting his beautiful sleep.

"Just ... interested I guess." Darrio's palm rubs back and forth against my arm as he holds me close.

"Interested?"

People are just *interested* in group sex? Really?

"Yeah, I—I want to know what it feels like. I want to know what they make you feel like."

34

"So … it's a competitive thing?"

A smile pulls at his lips and it makes my heart melt. He's so raw and handsome. Sometimes I wonder if he only smiles for me.

A self-centered part of me hopes he only smiles for me.

"No, not like that." He pauses as he studies my eyes. "I want to—" It seems difficult for him to talk about this but he's trying so hard. I make sure I don't push him. I let him tell me what he's feeling, and I love that he's telling me what he's feeling. "I guess I want to watch some other guy make you come. Watch the way he makes you shake and cry out. And then I want to fuck you better. To make you feel so good you can't even think about what he made you feel." His lips part but nothing comes out for a few seconds. "That sounds screwed up doesn't it? Maybe it *is* a competitive thing."

He seems confused and maybe a little embarrassed but I'm so turned on by the honesty of his words I can't speak.

"Would you say something, Kara? I feel awful right now. We don't have to do that. I didn't mean to make it sound like that." He's babbling and nervous and I've never seen Darrio like this. "Shit, I'm sorry."

"I want that too," I say in a rush.

The gray in his eyes swirls into a color of iron and power as he looks at me with a wide and astonished stare.

"Fuck, let's wake these assholes up right now." He rolls to turn away but I grip his shirt collar and pull him back to me.

His dark brows lower as he waits for me.

"Not yet."

I curl into him, hiding my face in the smooth scars of his chest.

A few silent seconds pass. He doesn't press me for answers. He doesn't ask a single thing. He just wraps his arms around me and holds me. He cradles my body until I fall back to sleep.

If Loki tests us today, if a war comes, if it all takes our lives away as if we're nothing more than dust, I want to make sure we spend our time together simply.

I don't want Darrio to worry about sex, and don't want Dax to worry about my life, and I don't want Ryder to worry about whatever it was those Travelers showed him.

I want peace.

If only for a moment.

Chapter Four

Mimicking

An anxious rhythm consumes my heart. It's a quick beat that makes me pace through our enormous room. My boots echo nicely against the cobble floor. When the soles of my shoes scuff over a black boot I look up to meet Ryder's worried gaze.

"Stop stressing. It's not a good look on you." He has the nerve to wink at me and I shove at his bicep, not letting my fingers linger against his smooth skin for too long.

He catches my wrist and pulls me against his chest. My feet stumble but he catches me, enveloping me into his warmth until I really do relax just slightly.

"They're going to test us. The gods don't give away their charity. But you're not just any Hopeless fae." His fingers brush against my jaw before pushing back my hair from my face.

His earnest eyes shine down on me. He has more faith in me than even I do.

"You guys know Kara's a sort of fire fae?" He doesn't

look to Darrio or Dax as he says it.

"Really?" Darrio steps closer, studying me intently.

I shift in Ryder's arms.

Daxdyn wanders over slowly, looking me up and down for several seconds.

"She doesn't act like a fire fae." A line forms between Dax's brows.

"And how do fire fae act?" Darrio shoots Dax a hard glare, and I'm just happy all their brooding and concerned looks aren't on me for a moment.

"Well, to put it nicely, you're kind of an overbearing, overly aggressive, arrogant asshole." Dax bites his cheek, and I can tell he's putting real effort into holding back his laughter.

"That's putting it nicely?" Darrio's big arms fold across his wide chest.

I can't help but wonder what happy insults I've missed out on during the last two hundred years of their lives.

"I'm just saying you guys hold a special sort of outlook on life, and Kara," Daxdyn's gaze softens when he looks at me. It's a look that sinks right into me. "Kara just isn't like that."

In Daxdyn's eyes I'm not an asshole ... what a delusional sense of love we must be in.

"I agree. I thought the same thing." Ryder's palm splays wide against my lower back. He holds me close as he considers this puzzle that is my life.

"What do you think it is?" Daxdyn asks.

"It could be anything really," Darrio says as he tilts his head to the side in thought.

"Excuse me, but the *it* that you three are picking apart right now is me. I'm a real fucking person and I'm right here. Don't ignore me like I'm not here."

Ryder's hand pushes lower until it's settled against my ass. His hard body is even closer to mine.

"I'm very aware you're right here, beautiful." His voice hums with a lustful sound.

With a roll of my eyes, I shove out of his arms.

These three are insufferable. They were thinking with their brains for all of five minutes before their dicks chimed back in.

"Hey, I was kidding." Ryder's fingers skim mine just before I fold my arms across my chest.

"This is serious. The mortal realm could very well depend on my magic. What the gods are offering us will definitely depend on this magic."

"Let me help you then." Ryder steps closer to me and confusion clouds my mind as he wraps his arms around me once more.

It's hard to be mad at him. He's patient, and sexy, and kind.

"Snuggling me is going to help somehow?" I don't unfold my arms to him even though I secretly love the way he feels pressed against me.

"Hmm, it couldn't hurt." A primitive sound hums through his chest and the corner of his lips tip up in a smirk. "I think your power is something else."

"Something else?" Dax leans his shoulder against the wall as he gets comfortable. He's still shirtless. The other two men have sadly put on their shirts while Dax lets the morning sunlight skim across the etched lines of his abdomen.

"When I worked with Mesa at the Iron Bar a few years ago, she told me about this fae she met there. She said he was *heavens blessed*. Different than the others. Not in appearance, but in power." Ryder's attention is held intently on the depths of my eyes. Darrio steps closer once more.

My nerves tingle through me, my magic swirling until the anxiety makes me feel like I might throw up.

"Stop being mysterious and tell me what you're thinking." My gaze narrows on his pale eyes.

"I think you have the ability to mimic others."

"Mimic?" Darrio cocks a brow at Ryder.

All the repetitive words are making the anxious energy grow within me. I swallow down the nervous feeling churning my stomach.

"Fae have special powers. Some have a few special traits, but not an abundance. I can shudder and I can heal, but that's it. That's all I have to rely on in life. Other than my charm, of course." Another cheesy wink has me groaning with annoyance. "But when you did your fire show, you were worried about Dax and Darrio." A small pause fills his voice. "They were probably all you were thinking about."

Finally, I do release my arms, letting them linger against his chest. The steady beat of his heart meets my fingertips.

"That wasn't all that was on my mind," I say quietly. The building angst between Ryder and I kept my mind busy when I wasn't worrying over Darrio and Daxdyn every waking hour.

A knowing smile consumes his features. Lines crease his pretty eyes making a fluttering energy course through my chest.

"Right, right, Ryder's glorious junk was also on your mind. Can we get to the point here?" Daxdyn shoots me a taunting look and I glare back at him from over my shoulder.

"I think she has the ability to mimic someone's power. I don't know if she has to be thinking of them or has to have made contact with them. It could be anything really, but we have a little bit of time to figure it out." Once again, Ryder pulls me closer, making my body align with every inch of his.

"You really think I could shudder just because I'm pressed up against a shuddering fae?"

"Well I hope you wouldn't take just any shuddering fae." Ryder dips his head low, his lips just a breath away from mine.

"I don't know, my current shuddering fae's ego is too big for me to really wrap my arms around him."

His tongue rolls slowly across his lips.

"Mmm, tell me again how I'm too big for you to wrap yourself around."

"Seriously?" Darrio cocks a brow at his friend.

"Is there possibly a less disturbingly sexy way for you two to do this?" Daxdyn says with little interest in the matter.

A smile pulls at the corner of my mouth for a moment before I really focus on what he just told me. If I put all of my thoughts into someone else's powers, could I really mimic them?

He keeps his palms firmly against my hips and ever so slowly he starts to flicker out of focus. His touch feels like waves drifting back and forth against my skin. His magic is strong. It's something that shivers right through me like a current.

"You sure that's safe, to have your magic going through her?" Dax suddenly seems concerned. The steady stride of his boots leads him over to me once again.

His palm brushes against my side, his thumb sweeping back and forth over my hipbone.

He's so careful with me now. Since we were separated he's done nothing but worry over me, it seems like.

"I'm fine, Dax." I force myself to look away from the depths of his silver eyes.

Daxdyn's hand slips away but he doesn't step back.

My eyes close and I focus on the shuddering feel of Ryder's hands on my body. The tingling feel of his magic is all I can think about.

"Don't lose focus, Kara." Ryder's voice holds warning.

"I won't."

"Good. There are some bad cases of shuddering fae being distracted when using this magic."

My eyes peek open to look up at the somber prince.

"What happens if I'm distracted?"

The weight of his gaze sinks right through. It sinks low until it's heavy at the bottom of my stomach.

"Sometimes nothing. Sometimes a hand or just a finger is lost during the teleportation."

"A finger?" It's a shrieking sound that leaves my lips. "I have three boyfriends. I need *all* of my hands."

I jerk my hands away from him and step back.

"Yeah, she's not fucking doing this." Dax follows me as I start to pace the room again.

My footsteps sound through the room. Dax's footsteps mirror mine. My pacing becomes a little quicker. Dax's pace follows suit. I turn around on the balls of my feet. Dax does not.

The smooth panes of his chest collide with my breasts.

"Do you mind?"

Can a woman not have a simple anxiety attack in peace?

"Kara, you can do this. I wouldn't have suggested it if I didn't think you were strong enough." Ryder holds his hand out to me invitingly.

Darrio nods, his brows pulled low over his intense gaze.

With minor hesitation, I step past Daxdyn and place my hand into Ryder's. The warmth of his palm pulls me closer until he wraps me up in his arms.

His strong heartbeat pounds against my chest, strumming strength into me.

The coarse feel of the sides of his head meet my fingertips as I stare up into his eyes. The light in the room falls across his gaze, making his eyes the color of the morning sky.

"How do I know where I'm going?" It's a quiet question. It's a sound of my fears rising up and strangely enough, I'm okay with these three seeing me at my weakest.

"Just think of a place. Or a person. Imagine it with vivid detail. Your magic will do the rest." He pauses for a second, searching my eyes intently. "Ready?" It's a whisper that fans across my lips.

"I am now."

I might always be ready as long as these three men are by my side.

As he starts to fade away, flickering in and out, I keep my eyes locked on his.

I think about the feel of his drifting form beneath my fingertips.

I think about the powerful buzz of magic pooling through me.

I think about the nerves in my body mimicking what Ryder's doing.

And then, at the last moment, I think of who I want to see right now.

I'm gone before I even realize it.

Chapter Five

A Game of Gods

Shuddering isn't at all the way it feels when Ryder guides me through space and time. There's no pain or anxiety. It's freeing and euphoric and consuming.

I honestly don't know why Ryder walks anywhere. This is the most addicting feeling I've ever felt.

Gentle winds kiss my skin but I don't feel whole. It's as if my mind, body, and soul have turned to dust and I'm just caught up in the wind somewhere in an unseen space. I'm aware of the quick movements of my travel but I can't see anything. Darkness blinds me to the world around me.

Until I land.

Ryder's gaze is alive with excitement.

"You did it," he whispers.

The quiet sound of his voice echoes around the arched hallway. Morning sunlight warms my back and before I can turn around he's speaking.

"You are a remarkable little thing, aren't you?" Loki's emerald eyes flash with interest. "I am curious which god blessed you so. I do have my guesses though." He leans against an artfully sculpted column, his back to the deep green field behind him.

"Perhaps I'm deserving of my gifts." My chin tips up to him.

Loud and unrepressed laughter shakes through him. The sound of it hums around the hall until he's doubled over laughing.

He stands to his full height. A smile still creases his features as he stalks closer to me. Ryder doesn't move but I feel his chest lean into me, brushing against my back.

"What sort of help do you require from the gods? Although I *do* feel someone has already helped you enough." His long fingers strum against his chin as he studies me with rapt attention.

I try to think of all the people in Juvar who will be harmed first. Then the villages past the sea. And then the world and realms beyond that will be destroyed because of Tristan.

He's invincible. I stabbed him through the heart twice and still he's a threat with too much power.

Dark magic is all that will stop that man.

"I want death magic."

Death. What an awful thing to ask for.

Loki's brows raise high but he never looks away from me.

"Death magic. You think gods would willingly hand out such a powerful energy? *And you didn't even say please.*" He shakes his head in disappointment.

My lips part and I consider adding the word as an afterthought, but it seems low and taunting of him to ask.

So I say nothing instead.

"What makes you think such magic exists?" His gaze flickers across my features.

I have no idea if death magic exists. Death is real. Magic is real. It is very possible that death magic is real as well.

"Are you saying it does not?" I'm careful with my words.

Birds chatter quietly in the serene distance just as a humming laugh skims across Loki's lips. He leans closer until his eyes narrow on mine.

"What are you willing to give for it?"

Anything.

Anything but Darrio, Dax, and Ryder.

"Would you fight for it?" Loki's shifting gaze is

magnetic and sparking with mischief.

Ryder's palm pushes up my arm.

"Kara, maybe—" Ryder's quiet voice is cut quickly off by my own.

"Yes."

Lightning flashes through the god's eyes.

I could never have anticipated the following few seconds.

Raw power shakes the ground, the polished cobblestone breaks away beneath my boots. The sky itself tears open, ripping away the world around me.

The silence and pretty scenery pulls away like a curtain revealing a stadium of chanting gods and goddesses surrounding us.

Intricate details of gold line the high brick walls of the stadium. The mark of the Hopeless creates arrows down the center of the walls in blood red colors.

"Welcome, my glorious friends," Loki's says with a wolfish smile. The amplified tone of his voice carries through the crowd and they cheer louder from the simple introduction. "I have a special treat indeed this morning." He claps his hands together as he looks to me and Ryder. "In just a few seconds two more guests will be arriving, do try to forgive their tardiness."

My brows crease.

Rumbling screams sound far off but begin to grow closer. Darrio lands hard at my feet, the dirt billows up around his form as he winces from the fall.

A gasp pulls from my lips but then the familiar sound of screaming fills the air once again.

I peek up at the pale blue sky just in time to see Daxdyn dropping from up above as well. Ryder's warm palm wraps around my waist and he pulls me back just in time. Daxdyn lands in a dusty heap at his brother's side.

"Fucking gods," Dax says under his breath.

The two fae stand slowly. Darrio's silver eyes shift over the roaring crowd. Dax dusts himself off.

"You didn't land like that did you?" Dax asks. Worry lines his brows as he's fingers skim across the inside of my palm.

"No. Not at all like that."

"Good." He nods his head as if everything is going according to plan here.

Everything is fucking perfect here in the beautiful Realm of the Gods.

"We have a great show planned for you all today."

Loki's booming voice echoes as his smile widens. His gaze collides with mine just as fear crawls all through me. "May the mayhem commence."

A sweeping bow is added with dramatic flair and I'm still staring at the peculiar god as doors at the far end of the colosseum rise. The walls shake as the wide doors pull back to reveal dark creatures.

Loki gives me a quick wink before he disappears like ash in the wind. The dark flecks of his features swirl out of sight and I have to force myself to focus on the opposite side of the arena.

As the bright sunlight strikes across the creatures' faces I realize, they're a cursed sort of monster. Only their eyes are defined. The nose and mouth are just slick skin that seems fused together in a sickening way. The depths of their eyes shine crimson in the morning light.

An eerie sort of blood red evil flashes within their gazes, chilling me to the bone just as the creatures start to race toward us.

Chapter Six

Powerful Magic

My father's sword weights my hand familiarly. The simple feel of it makes my body react, throwing my posture into a position of defense.

Magic hums through me. It buzzes around my veins, reminding me that I have more to depend on than just a man-made weapon.

The men wait with tension held in their spines for the dozens of creatures to make their way closer. About a hundred yards separate them from us. With each passing second, nerves build higher in my body, my heart thundering until it's all I hear in my ears.

I'm not waiting for this.

My jaw tightens. I close my eyes and try my best to focus on what I just learned fifteen minutes ago.

In a shuddering flash I'm in the air, my body resurfaces just above the creatures and I shove hard until my wings burst free from my back. Like a vengeful Valkyrie, I raise my sword and slam it down on an unsuspecting creature. As I land, its inky fingers wrap around my upper arm as my sword lodges in its shoulder. Pain shoots through me. Its fingertips start to sizzle against my skin, burning into me like hot tar dripping down my flesh.

I wince before heaving back and railing my blade through its core. Its sparkling eyes flash but the strike doesn't deter the monster.

My lips purse as I realize the gods gave us unfair opponents. My powerful wings push down hard, raising me several feet in the air. With perfect aim I slice the blade down once more.

The creatures head topples off and bounces only once against the dirt. I can't help but watch it roll, keeping my eyes locked on the empty red orbs in its tumbling skull.

Cheers erupt from the crowd.

At least they have the decency to applaud us instead of mock us.

My attention skims the crowd and it only takes seconds to find the little shit. Loki's happy gaze locks with mine. He sits leisurely on the edge of the wall, closest to the action. A sweet wave is passed my way. A man at his side, Baldur, shoves him with a stiff movement, causing the trickster god to slide from his little perch on the wall. Loki's happiness slips from his glowering face just as he disappears from sight once again.

Baldur nods to me before turning his back on the chaos that is now my life.

I push away the tangle of blonde hair from my face. Pain stings through me as long arms wrap around me, colliding hard with my body before shoving me to the ground.

The air is knocked from my lungs. Everywhere that the creature's body touches mine is fiery pain.

Fire.

My palms burn of their own accord. The creature's face is featureless, only shining eyes blaze back at me. No mouth, no nose, no features what-so-ever. I pull my hand back from its chest and raise it to its eerie face.

With intensity, I shove my magic out in heaps of anger and power.

White flames blaze from my palm, raining fire across the creature's slick face.

Not a single cry of pain emits from the thing. It staggers back from me, its hands trying hard to pull away the flames consuming its face. Its skin starts to melt together, the hands becoming one with the head. White bone waves back at me as its arms begin to shake with frantic movements.

I have to force myself to look away from the bizarre and disgusting sight.

Daxdyn smashes his boot into one of the creature's skulls. It quickly turns to sloshing mush beneath the force of his boot. He pulls back from the deformed thing, his lip curling as he stares down on it.

Another one is held between Darrio's palms. Its long fingers push frantically against his biceps. Thick smears of black cover his skin from where the creature touches. Darrio's fingers fume as he pushes his palms together with too much force and I have to look away just as the creature's head starts to sink in on itself.

Another, one of only a few that are left, grips my throat with its stinging palm. In a flash Ryder is before me, flinging the thing off of me. He struggles with it for only a second. His fingers grip it jaw and he slams it hard into the dusty earth. Over and over again until its jerking movements halt entirely.

It seems almost too easy now. A little painful, but easy.

Trepidation tingles through me.

It's a feeling of warning. Something is not right here.

My gaze flickers to the trickster god once again. He's

standing on the opposite wall now, pacing on the thin ledge while he watches me intently.

What does he want?

I look up to see the final three creatures running toward Daxdyn. They're a small horde of hellions. Poor magical infused creatures that the gods must have dug up for entertainment this morning.

I'm done. I'm over today's entertaining act.

My wings carry me high in the sky and I dart down at an alarming speed. My blade arches above my head and I strike down on the creatures, slicing through all three torsos like water. My boots meet the earth once again, and as I land, I begin striding past the corpses. My boots stomp through the tar-like blood until I'm standing just below Loki.

My eyes narrow on his taunting smirk. I push my hair back once more just to find that dark, inky blood coats my hands and face. The crowd quiets and just as Loki opens his mouth to say some annoying little overly dramatic spew, I cut him off.

"I *do* hope you enjoyed this morning's entertainment."

His hands clasp together and he gives a slow clap for our performance.

"It was impressive indeed. It was just the opening act to another, of course." In a flicking flash he's right in front of me. His head tilts as he studies me. Magic dances recklessly in his eyes. "How far can you push yourself?"

I don't speak immediately. I consider his words, trying to find the real meaning.

"Can you mimic a god or only simple fae magic?"

"Would it frighten you if I could?" Pure confidence laces my words. My chin tips up a little higher.

"Frighten." Shaking laughter skims through his thin frame. "Not at all. Intrigued is all. You are a special little fae. *Human*. You were human only weeks ago. And now you hold fire in your hands as if Hella herself gifted it to you.

"Tell me, can you do this?" With an arch of his fingers, the crowd gives a consecutive gasp.

I turn just as Ryder starts to stumble forward. His gaze shifts back and forth as his legs bring him awkwardly toward us. Ryder's attention falls on me and he doesn't look afraid of the god who is controlling his body. Ryder looks ... carefully cautious of what he might give away. His features are blank, not a single look of interest passes over him.

Loki lowers his hands and Ryder's movements halt.

Someone steps closer in the stands of the stadium. I glance past Loki and my gaze lands on Baldur. His bulky arms fold across his bare chest as he watches quietly.

"Bring him forward. Show me what power you're capable of." Loki's words are a commanding test.

This god just waves his little hand and wants me to monkey see, monkey do?

"I don't want to control Ryder." I say it through clenched teeth.

It's the last thing I want to do. These three love me. If I can control them, that seems … terrifying. I don't want to be this all-powerful mimicking thing. I don't want to be something to fear.

Suddenly, I realize how simple of a life I really want.

I want a house, and a family, and quiet nights surrounded by the ones I love.

It's so boringly simple.

And yet, so unattainable.

"Kara, I think you should try." Ryder's voice brings my attention back to the crowd of people waiting to see if I can perform this morning's little trick.

"Think of it like a string. A string within you connecting to the thing you want. You want Ryder, yes?"

Loki's provoking voice is like a humming sound in my ear.

Tension floods my chest but I try to nod. I try to do what I know will benefit me, and the humans, and the fae and all the realms that are depending on me.

My hand rises and I can't help but look to Darrio and Daxdyn over Ryder's shoulder. They don't appear afraid of me. Maybe I'm just overthinking this.

Or maybe, I'll turn into another of the gods' creatures.

With an arch of my fingers, I try to imagine a delicate string from my chest to Ryder's. It's strangely easy to imagine. It's easy to imagine my heart connected to his.

Because it is.

Overbearing magic pools within my chest. It's so powerful it hurts. A tingling sensation exits my body and, as my eyes open slowly, I see Ryder taking a staggering step closer to me. My heart leaps at the sight of it. Another few steps are all I demand of him before my hands clasp over my lips, hiding the shaking gasp that's slipping from me.

I force my hand to my side and smooth my features into a look of casual interest.

I try hard to keep my composure. I don't know why

I'm practically breaking down in the one place I should be most careful in.

Ryder strides the final few steps that separate us and he wraps me up in his arms in an instant. He hides my face in his chest just as a shaking exhale trembles through me.

I'll never let him know the terrible thoughts that are washing through my mind right now.

I'll hide it away to protect him.

To protect them all.

"You're so fucking amazing," he whispers against my ear as his fingers thread through my hair and he holds me close.

I'm not amazing though.

I'm *dangerous.*

Chapter Seven

Another Kind of Magic

I keep my hands intently to myself that night. I don't even consider testing my magic further.

Loki promised us one more surprise tomorrow.

Surprises from the gods aren't at all the sort of surprise you'd ever want.

The men are downstairs in a grand hall eating more food than I've ever seen. But I'm not hungry. And I can't stomach sitting on display for these gods for a single second longer.

So I lie alone in our room, dwelling on what tomorrow will bring. The soft blankets are comforting. If my mind could shut off, I'd probably fall asleep early tonight.

Not that that'll happen.

The door slowly pushes open. I sit up slightly and Daxdyn peeks his head in, his pace is slow as he enters. Hesitantly, almost.

"How are you feeling?"

He takes his time coming closer, his steps scuffing lightly against the floor. Gently, he sits at the edge of the bed, a few inches away from me. My back is to him but I can physically feel his every move. His emotions are my own, amplified to a suffocating feeling of disquiet. My hands are locked around my knees as I lie quietly in thought.

Until now.

"I'm fine." He's been especially worried lately and I try not to make him any more concerned than he already is.

He shifts, crawling a little until he's just behind me. I peek at him from over my shoulder as his long fingers start to massage my neck.

"What are you doing?" My eyes flutter closed as the protests continue to leave my mouth. "You don't have to do that."

I make nothing easy. For some stupid reason I can't just let Dax take care of me. Even if it's all that I want.

His thumbs press hard, circling slowly down my spine in just the right way. My head tips back at the amazing feel of it.

"I can stop if you really want me to." His voice holds a smirking tone. It always does. No matter what, he's always happy. Or at least tries to be. He pretends to be.

It's one of the reasons why I love him. He tries to be his best self. He makes me want to be better too.

His lips press to the side of my neck as his thumbs run the length of my shoulder blades.

Daxdyn must have been a masseuse in a past life. A sexy, sexy masseuse.

"You want me to stop?"

"No." Again he presses his lips to the base of my throat, sweeping his tongue along my skin before sucking lightly.

A breathy sigh leaves my lips and I feel his energy mingling with mine. I feel his lust spiraling through me.

And then I'm not thinking about relaxation, or Daxdyn's hands on my body, or even sex for once in my life.

I'm thinking about the way his magic is pushing into me, making me feel more than I could ever feel on my own.

I don't know what Dax really feels. He once described it as a numbness. It still breaks my heart to imagine that. To think that he's a shell of a man walking around with a false smile on his lips.

So I try hard to mimic him. It isn't a power that holds much strength but I know for him it'd be powerful.

I take the lust swarming my chest, he's toying with it, pulling at the emotion to fuel his own, but I shove it into him. I take that wanting, tightening, demanding feeling that's residing in my core and I push it hard into him.

He stills against my back, his lips halt against my skin. I tip my head to the side, slowly to him, holding his steely gaze.

A look like I've never seen is in his eyes.

When he speaks, it's a rumbling but raspy sound.

"Was that you?" He searches my eyes.

I feel his heart hammering against my back and I nod slowly.

"*Fuck*," His words are silenced by the hard feel of his lips slamming against mine.

As his tongue flicks against mine I push even more of my coiling emotions into him until he groans against my lips.

He shoves me against the mattress, his body slipping over mine. My fingers thread through his hair and I can't seem to stop myself from giving him everything within me. A hazy, drunken feel of lust still lingers within my chest but I love the way it's turning him on so I keep giving, and he keeps taking.

The hard feel of his cock grinds against my center and I roll my hips against his. Another forceful push of my magic and I know what he feels. It's too much.

It always feels like too much when I'm with them.

"Fuck." He jerks back from me, breathing unsteadily as he tries to focus on his words. "I—I need you to stop before I fucking come in my jeans."

A smile pulls at my lips. Weirdly, I really want that. I suddenly want nothing more than for Daxdyn to come in his jeans.

"Fine." I kiss his smooth jaw before my lips meet the column of his neck. The salty taste of him meets my tongue and it only makes me want to taste every inch of him.

"*Fine*?" There's confusion in his voice as if he wasn't prepared for me to give up so easily.

He knows me too well.

Never trust a thief, Daxdyn.

I push against his chest until he rolls, lying flat on his back. A look of uncertainty creases his brows. I can't help but smile at him as I climb on top. My legs straddle his hips. I lean into him and his hands grip my hips hard. He meets me half way, sealing his lips to mine, and our bodies push and pull against each other.

I'll never get tired of kissing Daxdyn Riles.

Maybe it's because he feels less than most, but he puts more into it than I've ever felt.

I start to dump my wanting emotions back into him and he groans as I pull away. My lips trail against his jaw line. I rake my teeth slowly against his neck, my fingers pushing against his shirt as I start to lower myself down his hard body. The soft cotton of his shirt against the smooth warmth of his skin meets my fingertips. I shove at the material until my lips graze his abdomen. The etched lines of his stomach guide my tongue, kissing tenderly before sucking hard.

Harsh breaths are the only sound that lingers around us.

As I unbutton his jeans his fingers thread tightly through my hair as if he's preparing for what's to come.

I kiss slowly against the hard lines that veer down into his jeans. I push them down and his voice deters me for only a moment.

"What if the gods see?"

My palm strokes him from over his thin boxers and his head tips back, showing me the strong angle of his jaw.

"Then they'll see why I keep you around, won't

they?"

His quiet laughter dies as the smooth length of his dick throbs against my palm.

I kiss innocently against his thigh and he shifts beneath me. Lightly, I hold him in my palm, pretending to forget his dick entirely as I make slow work of licking up his hipbone.

"Kara." The tormenting sound of his voice makes me bite back my smile.

I stroke slowly up his hard length as I drag my teeth lightly against his cut stomach.

Still I keep his dick as an afterthought in my actions.

Another slow roll of my wrist has him rocking against my palm. The coiling energy within me is pent up and I make sure to push it all into him in one heaping shove.

"Fuck, Kara. Please." He holds my head in his hands, pulling my hair but not forcing me where he wants me most.

My name is a rasping sound that circles the room and sends a tingling feeling all through me. I love the angsty way he always says my name.

After a few more drawn out seconds, I push his boxers down his throbbing length. With a smile, I kiss the tip of his dick. I hold his gaze and he's committed to holding my hair back to see every second. His rapt attention burns across my features. My tongue swirls over the smooth tip, taking my time tasting him. As my lips wrap around his length, gliding down him as far as I can go, he gives a growling groan.

My palm works up and down his shaft until his tip hits the back of my throat. My eyes flutter closed as my thighs shift, thinking about him there, hard and throbbing. I refocus that coiling energy back into him. I feel it flood through him and he fists my hair hard as his hips thrust against my mouth.

And after only a few short minutes, warmth seeps across my tongue and he stills beneath me. I suck hard making his breath even more ragged when I swallow.

"Fuck, that was embarrassingly quick." He releases my messy hair and pushes his hands over his face.

I lick up his shaft before rolling my tongue across my swollen lips, and he watches my every move with hooded eyes.

"That—" He pulls at my hand, bringing me down against his chest. His lips press slowly against mine. His eyes are wide with amazement. "I make you feel all that shit?"

I nod. "So much more."

He groans.

"Never do that again." Another slow kiss presses to my lips.

"What?" I can't help but kiss him back, the demanding energy in me swirling once again. "Why not?"

His arms wrap around me as his tongue flicks leisurely against mine.

"Because if that's how good I make you feel, I don't ever want you to give it away." His eyes hold mine. "If I had known that's what it really felt like for you, I would have made it my job to fuck you every single day. Promise me you'll never give that feeling away. Don't waste it on me. Promise me you'll keep it for yourself."

A small smile tilts my lips as he kisses me like I mean the world to him.

I make no promises though.

Chapter Eight

A Mistake

The following morning, I don't wait to see what spectacular game Loki is plotting. Once everyone is ready, I take Darrio's big hand in mine. Ryder grips Daxdyn's shoulder and with a simple nod we vanish from the quiet bedroom.

A cloud of dust storms around me as the four of us land in the arena from yesterday. The crowd is small but it is still early. They gather, taking their seats as a few of them point down at the four fae who wait with a ready stance for whatever the day might bring.

Unfortunately, Loki is nowhere in sight. Baldur, *unfortunately*, is.

With leisurely steps, he strides over to the four of us.

"You're a little early this morning." His gaze seems permanently held on me.

"I didn't particularly care for the way my men were escorted yesterday." My jaw locks shut as I tip my chin up at the god.

A small smile creases his features.

"My brother does have a flair for the dramatic."

What is Baldur's story?

What pawn is he in this play?

"I hope you've prepared for today." His features smooth into a serious look that almost makes me regret wasting my night blowing Dax instead of preparing.

Well, can't win them all I suppose.

"Of course we've prepared." Confidence tinges my voice even as a coughing laugh shakes through Daxdyn.

"Good. Then you'll have absolutely nothing to worry about."

"Absolutely nothing." I'm a fucking parrot of false confidence right now.

"Good luck." He nods politely, genuinely even. "I hope you get the help the mortals need, Zakara." His words are spoken so pointedly it sinks suspicion right through me.

Only when he's several feet away does anyone speak.

And it is, of course, a question of utmost importance.

"You think he wants to fuck her?" Dax asks under his

breath.

"At first, I did. Now I have no fucking idea." Ryder's tone holds confusion that I feel deep within myself even.

Half an hour of dwelling on it is all I'm allowed.

Loki flashes in with that annoying sneer of happiness.

"Good morning, my little fae. I'm pleased to see you here so early and *prepared.*" A very obvious wink is passed my way.

My lips curl at the hinting sound of his voice.

Loki is the one watching us.

Well, I hope he enjoyed the show. He must think I'm really powerful making Dax come that fast. Yes, I really use my magic for the better good.

I don't know what he gains from watching us.

I originally thought it was a perverted set up, and now I'm wondering if it's just another game for the gods. A ploy to study us, watch us, and mock us.

"We actually have rather important things to be doing in the mortal realm. If we could just move along with the day's *festivities.*" My hands plant firmly on my hips.

"Oh, I do like your enthusiasm." He nods a manic

shake of his head. "This morning, I thought I'd go a little easy on you. Give some of you a break."

With a wave of his wrist the three men at my side disappear. I gasp, hating how this god has the ability to rip away the only happiness I have in my life.

Yells coast through the air and I know what's happening before I see it. Daxdyn, Darrio and Ryder land in pile within the stadium of the colosseum. An older woman gasps at the sight of the men lying at her feet. Her lip curls as if they're pigeon droppings instead of a mound of sexy fae men.

With annoyed looks lining their faces, they stand. Ryder brushes off his jeans and I see Dax mumble something but they're too far away from me to hear.

"Your men are impressive. The finest ones you could have chosen. But we all know you are the one holding this war together. If you want help from the gods, you must earn it yourself." His eyes narrow on me and before I can even reply, he's gone. The wind sweeps him away. I turn, searching the seats for the tormenting god.

He stands with a pleased smile pressed to his lips, right next to Darrio, Daxdyn, and Ryder.

Darrio stares hard at the side of Loki's face. I can see it in his stormy eyes; he's plotting the god's death.

If anyone possessed the rage to murder a god, it'd

probably be Darrio.

The doors at the far end of the gate are still closed. Gods and goddesses continue to take their seats. I have five minutes at least.

Small puffs of dirt billow up from my stalking steps as I make my way over to the three men watching me intently.

"You're going to do fine," Ryder says with assuredness. He leans against the edge of the brick, his arms folding as he stares down at me in my little shit hole pit.

"I know. I'll be fine."

Daxdyn looks less convinced. Honestly if he just pretended to believe in me, it'd really help.

"Thanks for the burst of confidence, Dax." I glare up at him, the sun hitting my eyes and shadowing his smooth features.

"You'll do fine," he echoes in a quiet voice. He looks like he wants to wrap me up in a safety blanket and never let me go.

"Thanks." I shake my head at him and just as I'm about to walk away a deep rumbling voice pulls at my attention.

"Whatever comes out of that gate isn't a match for

my fucking human."

My head tips up to starry eyes. Darrio's gaze skims to my lips before trailing to the scar against my neck.

I know he's just saying it to boost my confidence, but he also knows I'm not the headstrong, breakable human I was just a few weeks ago.

I might be immortal for all we know.

And I guess we're about to find out.

The walls shake as the gate at the far end of the arena opens. It pulls back like the mouth to hell. The simple sight of it makes my heartbeat kick up into an impossible speed. Magic swarms my veins, prepared for whatever horde of creatures Loki has prepared today.

My fingers wrap one by one around the hilt of my sword. With swift movements, I pull the blade from my belt. My spine stiffens as my eyes lock onto the open space within the walls.

I search every inch of the shadows for what lies beyond.

Nothing.

Nothing is there.

No rushing creatures scurry from the darkness to attack me.

My sword lowers and I take a single step forward.

When his massive bare foot hits the dirt, dread sinks through me. It's nearly the size of my arm. An odd coloring clings to his flesh, like blood is laying forgotten and thick just beneath his dry skin.

Tattered jeans are all he wears and when his gaze meets mine, I nearly vomit. His crumbled and beaten skull is sunken and deformed, but he stares back at me as if he feels nothing.

The man's strong build nearly fills the wide expanse between the walls. He slowly walks forward, taking his time and peering up at the roaring crowd with confusion in his blue eyes.

"My glorious friends, thank you for joining us this morning." Loki's introduction is a bit later than I expected. "Our one and only, Druw was available for entertainment today. For those of you who don't know," Loki's attention falls to me, an amused smile clings to his lips, "Druw was once a fae who came to me for help."

My stomach turns and I step back to get a better look at the god. My shoulder's hit the far wall as I look up at the god of mischief and realize what a terrible mistake I have made.

"Druw was a fae who came to me and asked for

everlasting life." The crowd chimes in with laughter at just the right time and Loki soaks up their adoration. "And so, after winning a few tasks I set before him, I granted his request." With every word Loki speaks, terror shakes through me. This was a mistake. "I granted him everlasting life just as mankind was starting to bloom. And look at him now, prospering from my gifts. Isn't that right, Druw?"

Druw looks lifelessly up at the god with a glazed and possibly blinded eye. He looks up at the god who granted him an endless and terrible life.

My hand shakes against the wall and I barely turn my back on the crowd before vomit spews from my mouth. It burns up my throat with vengeance.

My fingers fist in my palm and I bring it to my lips. I wipe away the mess and turn back to the god still smiling down on me.

"Druw, meet Kara." Loki instructs the fae with slow and annunciated words. Druw's hulking neck swings his head toward me unsteadily. "Druw, if Kara wins today, I'll grant her request, just like I did for you. Do you want that? *Do you want me to help her like I helped you?*"

As if those words trigger something in Druw's mind, the fae's enormous feet storm across the dirt. The dust billows up around his heavy steps like the start of a sand storm.

78

My wings expand without effort. They arch behind me, threatening to pull me from Druw's grasp if needed.

I raise my sword and my gaze widens as I realize how quickly he makes his way across the lengthy arena. I raise the blade and sweep it through the air just when he's near enough.

I put every ounce of strength into that blow.

I'm jarred when the fae grips the shining blade in his fist, stopping the attack with ease. Swollen blue eyes stare curiously at me. The left one is bloodshot and graying around the iris. This monstrous man is fisting my sharp blade as if it's nothing but an annoyance to him. For a second, I just gape at him. Until his fist tightens. With a tiny and insignificant move, he bends the length of my blade into an L shape.

An angry gasp falls from my lips at the sight of the angled blade.

"What the fuck?"

I jerk it away from his mammoth paws. The fae sways slightly as he stares down at me, blocking out the sun behind him.

Fury storms through my chest and with more anger than I've felt in years, I slam the bent blade through his bulky chest. I have to angle the attack in an unusual way because of the damage he's done on the beautiful blade.

Most of it sinks in. Stopping where the blade arches at a different angle. The hilt of it sticks out of him like a bent nail sunk into an old board.

Fucking dungeon troll.

I'm pouting and stomping around. I'm weaponless while I circle the most dangerous opponent the gods could have found for me.

Tristan had my blade in his possession for days and no harm came of it. This asshole touches it for a second and destroys it like a toothpick.

As Druw looks down at the blade plunged into his chest his features fall. More so than usual.

His lip curls, revealing nubs of rotted teeth. His gaze drifts to me and before I can even shield myself he grips my wing.

I lunge to run but he only tightens his grasp. The fine bones break beneath his powerful grip and I wince from the feel of the stabbing pain prickling down my spine.

With a growl, he hurls my body against the wall. My shoulder hits hard, my soft wings taking most of the impact. Grit scrapes against my bare shoulder, tearing slightly at the skin. My cheek stings against the blow and I know it'll bruise quickly.

A deep breath fills my lungs and I stand slowly on swaying legs.

Druw shakes his head and takes a few steps back, my blade still protruding from his chest. Not a drop of blood coats the wound.

"Druw," I take another short breath, realizing how much my lungs hurt, "I don't want to hurt you, Druw."

His wobbling head turns to me once more. A sadness is etched into the depths of his gaze. It's like it's pouring from him. It might be all he feels, if nothing else.

His footsteps pound against the dirt as he looms over me. With magic coursing through me, I shudder away from him. I take a moment to catch my breath as I play cat and mouse with an ancient corpse the gods have graciously kept alive.

He trails after me. From one flicking place to the next.

This is embarrassing.

I can't seem to kill him. I can only dodge him.

How will this end?

I lean against the far wall, my palm planted against the warm brick as I take another short but much needed break.

How did I get this out of shape?

I could use a nap.

A nap sounds wonderful right now.

Ryder and Daxdyn flicker in, scaring the hell out of me.

My heart pounds hard as I glare up at the two of them.

"Dax insisted I bring him down here." Ryder shrugs and I avert my glare to the fae at his side.

"I'm a little busy right now, Dax." I peek over his shoulder at my opponent who's stomping toward us.

"Busy playing hide and seek? When he gets his hands on you he's going to toss you around like an uninflated ball. You're just pissing him off."

"What do you suggest?" My lips purse together hard. I mentally calculate how much time we have before Druw gets here and tosses me around like a damn deflated ball.

"I suggest you start protecting your core a little more."

My core?

He's worried about my core of all things?

I shove my hair back from my face and then stop,

not moving an inch as his words circle my mind.

"Thanks, Dax." My lips barely brush the angle of his jaw before I shudder away once more.

My body becomes solid when I'm just in front of Druw, poised a few feet above him. Channeling Loki's magic, my fingers arch against the breeze and I pull him off the ground slightly, making him meet me half way. I put as much strength as I possess into slamming my body down on him. My boots meet the hilt of my sword tucked close to his abdomen, and I kick off hard from the weapon embedded in his chest.

And just as I had hoped, it tears through his abdomen. Right through his core.

The strong blade rips through the fae's internally rotting organs and they fall in a splattering heap between his feet.

He lands hard on his knees, sloshing the mess and stench of his organs. I swallow back the smell of it and force myself to finish what I started.

Thick, dark blood coats the hilt of the sword as I pick it up. My jaw clenches, my palms holding tight to the damaged blade in my hands. I sweep the sword up with a mixture of strength and powerful magic.

It slices up through his ribs. The muscles of my arms tense as I force the blade through his shoulders and neck. I step past him as he lands face down in the bloody dirt with a hollow sounding thud.

I shudder away from it all. Away from the applause and away from the lingering stench of a centuries old death.

Chapter Nine

The Gift of Sacrifice

I land hard in the grassy expanse of paradise that we first walked in to. My knees hit the soft ground and my stomach heaves. It forces up the pent-up smell of that fae's flesh and blood. For a few moments, my body rejects everything in my stomach until there's nothing left.

Ryder, Darrio, and Dax's boots stand around me, but I don't look up at them. I stay hunched over for a long while, breathing in deep breaths of the fresh and clean air. I slowly pull my wings in, knowing they'll heal faster within me. My body becomes weighted with the magic caressing the wings within.

Darrio lowers himself, his palm pushing up and down my spine.

No one speaks.

They let me dwell on my choices and my actions.

Until he arrives.

"Congratulations." Loki's voice sounds entirely too pleased.

I wipe my mouth with the back of my hand and I stand to face the demented god before me.

"No one has beaten Druw ... *ever*." Wide eyes wait for me to claim my prize.

It would be a cursed prize.

It was already a dark thing to ask for.

Death magic won't save us. Especially *cursed* death magic.

Whatever Loki gives me will not be a gift at all.

I'd end up just like that fae who asked for eternal life and got it.

"Thanks." I step back from him, my shoulder hitting Ryder's chest.

"Are you ready to receive your request?" He holds his hands out, waiting to give me just what I asked for.

Baldur and Viola shudder in at Loki's side, but neither of them speak. The three of them wait patiently.

This was a waste of time. We gained nothing by being here. I screwed up once again.

"I think we're ready to leave," I say carefully.

Daxdyn nods continuously like it's the smartest thing I've ever said.

Loki's eyes flash with interest. It's like seeing lightning strike through the darkest night.

"You are an interesting little mortal, Zakara Storm." His fingers lace together. "I don't think you are the type of woman to change her mind. But know this, you will never have another chance at the destroying power I could give you. And you will *not* win this war without that kind of power."

His thin lips tip up into a haunting smile just before the wind carries him away. His features flake away like ash until he's gone entirely.

Regret swirls through my chest.

I had a chance at power that would end this war before it had even begun, and I passed for my own selfish reasons.

"It isn't selfish." Viola's soft tone demands my attention.

It is selfish. If I had the nerve to let Loki's magic destroy me from the inside out, then everyone's lives would be simpler.

"You haven't even considered if there is someone else who would help you." Baldur's deep tone has hidden meaning.

I peer up at the beautiful man before me. Is he really

as kind as he seems? Or is he the same as Loki?

"What is it you want, Baldur?" My arms fold across my chest, and despite his kind appearance, I can't find it in me to trust him willingly.

"I want nothing." He shrugs his wide shoulders. Still I stare daggers at him. "There are some mortals we relate to on a deeper level. There are some we want badly to help even if we cannot." His attention, as always, is solely on me. "Your path is much like my own. Sometimes fate rests a little heavier on some people's shoulders than others. I wish it was different for you. I wish life was different. I see that familiar struggling ambition within you. It's there because your father is not. You have the will to win this war, but not the power."

His words hit hard within me.

He's right. I know he is.

"So help me." It's a quiet and pleading request.

His eyes soften as he looks at me as if he'll never see me again.

"I already have."

Confusion and shock storm through me. My lips part but he doesn't let me speak.

"Take a walk with Viola. It'll calm you."

A walk. With my boyfriend's ex. Yes, that sounds very relaxing.

"Come, Zakara." Her whispered words are not a question at all. And she doesn't wait as she starts to walk up the path ahead.

Darrio and Daxdyn exchange glances and I look to Ryder for a hesitating second before following after Viola.

A winding path of smooth bricks guides our way. A sparkling effect gleams off the bricks as the warm sunlight shines down. The ends of Viola's thin dress sway against the ground as we walk and I find myself comparing our differences.

She's soft curves with a deadly smile. Alluring but terrifying all at once.

Not a thing like me.

Or so I tell myself.

Small white flowers dot down the braid that's pulled over her shoulder. When she turns to me, I hold her gaze, my head tipping higher.

A stupidly strong sense of confidence streams through me as I hold the powerful goddess's gaze.

"We've been watching you." Her eyes shine with an unseen smile.

The eerie statement doesn't chill me like it should. I've always known the gods watch us. Especially now. Perhaps not as closely as they should. For if they did, my father wouldn't have died protecting me.

The gods do not do their jobs as sufficiently as they should.

"And what have you seen?" I don't cower away from the power I feel rolling off of her small frame.

Her attention drifts over my features as her head begins to shake back and forth.

"A headstrong child who grew up to be a headstrong woman." Her hands fold in front of her as she starts to walk farther into the beautiful, blooming garden. "A damaged woman unsure of herself, but so sure of the world around her. A beautiful fae who can't seem to make a choice between the most loyal of men."

Her simple assessment of my life sets my nerves into an angry frenzy.

So she watched me and judged me. She doesn't understand the feelings I've felt. The love and loss I've experienced.

"There will be more." At the sound of her vague statement, I stop in my tracks.

"More what?"

"There will be more love and loss to come, Zakara."
The glinting look in her eyes makes my heart stumble. "I
haven't felt your feelings, no. But I *do* know what your
path will bring." Her detached smile makes my jaw
clench tighter. How can she be so happy as she tells me
more lives will be lost? "There's a fire within you. And
there is magic to match it."

I try to find some source of help in her words.
Something. There must be something this infuriating
woman can give us to assist this helpless cause.

"It isn't helpless. Nothing ever is. You of all people
should know that. The Hopeless will always know that."

I hate how much she's in my head, forcing me to
rethink all my thoughts before they're thought.

"Do you want my help, Zakara Storm?"

Pushing aside my irrational irritation, I nod.

Her hand extends to me, palm up toward the deep
blue skies.

White, fuming smoke drifts through the air, pooling
within the palm of her outstretched hand.

Crisp white. The color of the heavens. A sign of
purity. The symbol of innocence. Nothing at all ominous
or threatening.

And yet, the magic within my veins scurries away

from it, demanding I step back from the gently swirling smoke.

"What is that?" My gaze never leaves the magic in her hand.

"It's the Gift of Sacrifice."

Caution is all I have with these gods.

"What does it do?" My uncertainty wavers through my tone.

Her eyes flash with unseen power.

"I shouldn't offer you anything. You've been blessed more than any other. I shouldn't even offer you prayers of safe travels, let alone something as powerful as this."

Hesitation fills my chest, pushing up my throat and keeping me silent.

Ryder trusts this woman. He asked for her above all others.

"Do you want it or not?"

She hasn't tormented us the way Loki has. She's been kind. Even if I thought she'd be awful, she was nothing but polite to us.

I swallow hard, and I'm speaking before I can even second-guess the danger of the gift.

"Yes."

A malicious smile parts her lips and her palm slams against my chest so fast I barely see it. Fire burns through me, swarming my lungs and drilling through me hard enough to make me gasp a painful breath.

And then … total euphoric energy tingles through my veins before settling warmly in my heart.

The Gift of Sacrifice.

It's just as painful and beautiful as it sounds.

Chapter Ten

New Haven

Viola's wide eyes eat up my every changing emotion.

"It hurts, yes?"

I'm still wincing as the energy swirls calmly in my chest.

Fucking goddess asking if it hurts as if she's ever felt a drop of pain.

"We feel pain, Zakara. Pain and pleasure and everything in between." The smooth sensation of her palm against my knuckles makes my spine stiffen. "Be the power that guides them. That inspires them. That saves them."

Darrio's heavy boots pull my attention away from her demanding words. His stormy eyes shift from my hand that I'm clutching to my chest to my other hand that's held in the goddess's.

"Everything … okay here?" Hard, shifting eyes take in her every move as if the fae might strike this powerful goddess down for causing me harm.

I remain hunched over, trying to find a breath of air.

"Everything is as okay as we can hope." A light lilt kisses her soft words.

Gods, why does everything she say make a demon want to claw its way up my throat with snarky, shitty retorts.

"Deep down, you're not as angry as you seem." She tilts her head at me and my awful thoughts. "These men bring out the best in you."

That —she is right about that.

Ryder and Daxdyn walk slowly up behind Darrio. Ryder's uneasy attention drifts between us, his hands held in his pockets.

Baldur steps up quietly, pushing past the three men. A small smile reaches his eyes. I stand to meet the intriguing god. I still don't know anything about Baldur, but I'm certain he's the closest thing to a friend that I have here. He doesn't speak a word as he pulls out what I thought I'd destroyed.

My sword gleams like new, catching the sunlight and shining it all around.

"My sword." I swallow hard as my fingers wrap around the hilt of it. The metal's smooth beneath my touch, as if it hasn't had a single taste of combat before.

"I thought you might … need it." His rumbling timber

is low and calming.

When I look up at him a smile is on my lips, and his kind gaze sinks right into me.

"Thank you."

Ryder, Darrio, and Dax all look at the god as if he's just offered me a glass of poison to drink down.

I clear my throat, shooting them all a glare hidden with a smile.

Their hard looks turn slowly away from the kind god.

Ryder shifts his attention even further, turning to Viola.

"There is one more thing, Vi."

Her pretty eyes settle on the prince.

"You want me to get your army into the mortal realm? All nine hundred and thirty-two of them. That's a small number in comparison. All the greatest wars had thousands at their disposal. Nations with as many as millions waiting to defend their country." She still holds my hand with a gentle touch.

"Well there's that dragon horse too." Daxdyn's voice trails off in thought.

"The gift of the gods rallied only nine hundred and thirty-two." That asinine smile of hers is still spread wide across her features.

Nine hundred and thirty-two. I've never thought so much about a number before. It is a small amount to win a war, but it is a massive amount to lose in a war.

But we're not setting out with the intention of losing.

"So, you'll send us then?" My gaze rises, meeting hers with intensity held in my eyes.

The smile softens, becoming more genuine.

Only a small second passes.

"Of course."

Finally. Finally, I like her.

Just in time for her to whirl us away.

***

The goddess's magic isn't like the chaotic shuddering power Ryder possesses. Maybe it's because we're being sent through realms instead of space, but I don't feel a single thing. Numbness sinks into me as a darkness fills my sight.

Until we're spit out on the other side. Nine hundred and thirty-two soldiers, one dragon horse, and a few Hopeless fae leaders land in a heap on the ground in the mortal realm. Pain stabs through my shoulder the moment I hit the earth.

Welcome back to the mortal realm. Enjoy your stay.

Rain pelts down from the dark, cloudy heavens. The sleet stings against my skin, and for a few seconds, I just lie there. Smoke fills my lungs just as it has my entire life in this world. I had forgotten about it. During my short stay within the beautiful Hopeless realm I'd forgotten the destroyed world I left behind.

"Let's set up in the clearing just over there." Darrio points toward an empty space among the forest, his head slightly downturned against the stinging rain. "Kara, do you know where we are? How far the kingdom is from here?" He kneels at my side as I lay in the mud at his feet.

I'm a defeated little pile of hopelessness. I was really aiming I'd go unnoticed for at least a few minutes.

Zero breaks. I'm beginning to find there are zero breaks when you're a leader.

Stiffly, I stand, attempting to look like the gift from the gods that they just spit out.

Through the heavy sheet of rain, I peer into the distance, trying to determine which way the smoke is coming from. The weather is harsh, but the sun always rises on the kingdom, it always shines down on the source of our destruction.

The sun is nearly setting now, it can almost be seen through the pounding rain and the heavy smoke and the dense clouds. Faint rays of white sunlight cut through the billowing, dark clouds.

"We're in New Haven. The coast is just to the east. Juvar is just beyond that." I point the way and his attention lingers in the distance as if he can see the fiery kingdom clearly.

New Haven. Of all the places Viola could have deposited us, she dropped us into New Haven.

There has to be a reason for it.

The cold rain tingles against my face as I peek up at the heavens.

"You okay?" Dax's long fingers tangle slickly with mine and he does a once-over of my body, seemingly checking for any damage from our fall.

His voice is sweet, concerned. It's too sweet, really. There's a reason Darrio is a commander and Daxdyn doesn't possess a single scar.

He isn't built for war.

Part of me wants to shield him from whatever tomorrow brings. He's capable. In a fight, his powerful strength can hold his own. But in a war ...

"I'm okay," I say in the quietest voice.

"Let's set up there." Darrio's orders cut through my thoughts. "We'll head to the sea once the storm passes. We're not risking our lives on a choppy sea filled with nix."

The nix. Are the creatures here already? So much time slipped by in the Realm of the Gods but hardly any at all has really passed. Time halted while we were there and now I have no idea what we're up against. I don't know if they've already consumed this world and moved on to the Hopeless realm, or if they're still building their strength in Juvar.

If they're here, I want to check on my people. The mortals are not safe here. They need distance between them and the death that's coming.

"I'm going on ahead." I meet Darrio's serious gaze. "I'm heading to the village near the sea."

My aunt's village.

"Those people need to be evacuated. They can't stay here. It isn't safe." I pause and Daxdyn nods in agreement, but Ryder begins to shake his head 'no' while Darrio just stares down on me. Darrio seems to be considering me intently.

"You're right," Darrio finally says as rain trails down his face and beard. "You and Ryder can shudder on ahead. The soldiers who have the ability will meet you there. Warn them, evacuate them. The rest of us will be right behind you."

I consider the small island of Juvar. The hundred or so innocent families who live within the kingdom. I was one of those innocent families when my father was alive. We lived there out of necessity for his job as a royal swordsman. There are only two types of people who dwell within the kingdom; privileged people who work for the king and people who are too poor to have a choice.

My stomach dips low, wishing they had a fighting chance in all of this. They're already gone though. Probably within the first hour Tristan arrived.

His own people. They never had a chance.

I swallow hard.

Ryder slips his hand through mine, pulling at my swarming thoughts. Water trails down our fingertips, and for a few seconds he only stares at me. Rain clings to his lashes, sliding down his face like tears.

Death can cause an ugliness to crawl out of all of us.

The Traveler's words echo in my mind as I stare up at the worry that lines his beautiful face.

What did he see in his travels?

He bends slightly, his other hand skimming up my

neck before cradling my jaw.

A questioning whisper hovers against my lips, unsure if it'll really be spoken because the answer will surely be avoided once again.

"Ryder, what did you s—"

His damp lips press gently against mine. The kiss silences my question. The sweetness of it consumes me with an aching fear that presses against my chest.

As my lashes flutter closed, his magic burns through me. I feel my body begin to fade.

I don't admit it, but I'm afraid I already know what he saw.

That fear clings to me as he rips us away from the world.

Chapter Eleven

Old Friends

We land in the middle of the village just in front of Saint's Inn; the most prosperous whore house in all the land. Or so my aunt says.

The rain soaks into me, chilling me as I stand clinging to Ryder, his lips hovering near mine as we just breathe each other in. I hate that we're avoiding something so big. I hate that he's keeping it from me.

Why would he keep it from me?

Deep down I know why.

"You two going to just cuddle all day or are we going to save the world and shit?" The gruff tone pulls my attention away from my dark thoughts.

I turn and I know who it is before my eyes even lock with his.

Fucking Streven.

"Being the second in command, I assumed you wouldn't need so much hand holding." My lips purse as I begin hiking through the mud to my aunt's house.

The weather darkens the empty street. Deep puddles line the lane of small, deteriorating houses. Shacks with minimal shelter surround Saint's Inn. Sleet beats against them, tapping hard to get inside the small homes.

But Saint's Inn stands shining and proud among the storm. Impenetrable from the chaos outside.

Until the nix come.

That thought has me moving faster.

"I thought the pretty little angel might need my assistance," Streven says, keeping pace with me as I jog across the muddy road. I don't have time for his banter right now.

Two more fae shudder in at my side.

"I need you to spread out, get the people out of their homes. Tell them to pack only what they can carry and to seek safety as far away from the coast as they can get." The porch steps meet my boots quickly as I storm up the stairs.

The four of them disperse. They head in all directions and a meager amount of calmness pushes into me just knowing we'll get this place cleared out soon.

Pain shakes through my knuckles as I bang hard

against the door. The small numbers 6969 above the door rattle against my force.

The door cracks open, not allowing the rain to come inside. A woman a little younger than myself peers out at me. Her amber eyes look up at me in confusion. My lips part, unsure how I should say this.

Finally, Lady Ivory steps into the hall behind the woman. Long blonde locks curl lightly around her pretty features.

"Kara, sweetheart!" My aunt's voice makes me weak. It makes the terror in me grow into an unmanageable thing.

What if something happens to these people?

They're so fragile.

"We have to go. I need you to get everyone together." I pause on the lacy bra the woman in front of me is wearing. "Get them dressed. In *weather appropriate* clothing. Something that'll cover more than her boobs would probably be best."

I push open the door and step inside. The two of them look at my drenched clothes and tangled, wet hair as if I'm a wild woman.

Maybe I am now.

"What is going on, Kara?" Lady Ivory pulls the beige

cardigan covering her small frame around herself, hiding the tight black corset beneath.

Her emerald eyes, identical to my own, grow wide with worry.

My gaze shifts to the woman at her side, not wanting to panic everyone all at once, but also knowing it's inevitable.

"Jaylee, gather everyone downstairs. If the upstairs guests are busy and unwilling to stop ... " A pause lingers on Lady Ivory's tongue. "Bang on the door and tell them you think there's been a minor outbreak of syphidia."

I arch a brow.

"Yeah, that might get their attention." My mumbled words go unnoticed.

Once Jaylee's footsteps fade away, I turn my attention back to my aunt.

"There's a war coming." Is that the best way I should be starting this conversation? Her lips part as her brows pull together. "Creatures, violent creatures, will be coming in from the coast of Juvar." The image of their claws shredding through my leather boots and flesh rips through my thoughts.

"When?"

I feel helpless. Power broods within me and still I

feel like I'm fumbling to save the ones I love.

"I don't know." It's a worthless answer. Not even an answer at all. "Soon, as soon as they can cross the sea. Within a day at most. I've brought help from the Hopeless realm but it isn't safe here. Get a bag packed and take these people as far west as you can go."

Her small palm runs down my arm, lingering against the inky Hopeless mark on the inside of my wrist.

She's never seen me as a fae. And yet, she doesn't question it.

Maybe she's always known.

"This is our home. Your father built me this house." She swallows hard as she looks back at the few women sitting in the dimly lit living room. They speak in quiet, murmuring tones but their eyes shift to me every few moments.

The warmth of the house starts to sink into me but it isn't enough. A shiver chills my skin.

"It's just a house, Ivory." I never knew my father built her this house. The memories she has of him as her brother must outnumber the few memories I have of him as my father. Does she cling to those memories the way I do mine?

"I'll get them ready, but I'm not leaving." Her long

hair sways as she tips her head up with refusal.

"Ivory … *Celeste* … " I breathe out her real name. One I've never actually used. It's what my father used to call her. Before she was an escort. "You can't stay here. He wouldn't want you to stay here."

Her gaze levels me. The look reminds me that she's the only person I care about in this realm. She's the only person I want to save and she's the only person who's going to be a pain in my ass about it.

"He wouldn't want me to leave you either." And she never has. She's always been here for me.

A mother when I didn't have one. A parent when there wasn't one. A friend when I needed one.

She's not going to leave me no matter how hard I try.

"If they come," *when.* When they come is the proper word, "I need you to stay in the cellar. Don't open it for anyone. Will you promise to do that?"

A smile almost pulls at the corner of her thin lips.

"Of course." She swallows before a real smile forms against her beautiful features. "If you promise never to use that name for me ever again." I breathe out a smirk and she turns from me before I can even reply.

In low, hushed tones she instructs the three women

who are sitting with perfect posture on the swooping settee against the living room wall. The small couch makes them look more delicate. Breakable.

I exhale a heavy breath and turn back to run out into the rain. My chest hits hard against Streven's and he looks down at me with a piercing gaze.

Something about him gets under my skin. A petty part of my mind wonders if it's because he's so close to Darrio. Or maybe it's just because he called me out when I wanted him to accept me. Darrio trusts him entirely.

I should too.

"Sorry," I say stiffly, stepping back from him with tension filling my spine.

"The village is packing up as we speak."

My eyes narrow on him despite how impressed I am.

There's a hundred people in this village at least. It took me five minutes to get one house moving.

"We don't dally when it comes to war, love." He pushes past me, into my aunt's home and I immediately want to push him back out.

To shove him and his coarse attitude away from my sweet, innocent aunt.

Her attention settles on his long, wild hair and wide shoulders, then trails down to his lean hips. Her heated gaze lingers on his hips for several long, uncomfortable seconds.

Okay, perhaps she's not so sweet and innocent. But she doesn't deserve his terrible attitude either.

With a wave of her hand, she ushers the women upstairs, hopefully to start packing.

I hope they pack more food than sexy underwear, but it may be a warning best left unsaid.

Streven strides through her home with overbearing confidence. His boots press heavily against the aged floorboards. Lady Ivory watches his every move.

"Streven." The appraising look in her eyes has me cocking a brow at her. My arms fold tightly across my chest.

How does she know him?

Okay I know exactly *how* she knows him, but really, how?

I told her five minutes ago that deadly creatures are threatening our lives. And now she's mentally measuring Streven's dick.

Typical.

"It annoys you how much alike you two are, doesn't it?" Ryder's voice whispers across my neck, sending a shiver down my spine.

My brows crease as I turn to him, and his warm palms settle against my hips, pulling me flush against his hard body. A coldness clings to our wet clothes but our bodies fight against it, warming each other in all the right places.

"We are not alike," I say in a harsh whisper.

A smirk pulls at his lips as he looks up at the hungry look that's filling my aunt's gaze.

His fingers skim beneath my shirt, tingling against my skin. His tongue rolls across his lower lip.

"You're sure about that?"

Discreetly, I shift my hips against his, making his gaze lower to my mouth as he leans in close. Until I deliberately pull back, putting cold air between him and I.

"I'm positive."

That sexy smile of his almost consumes me, almost has me pushing him against the wall and ignoring the outside world for just a few hours.

Instead, I walk away from him entirely.

Just. To. Prove. A. Point.

A hum that sounds slightly like a groan leaves him and I mentally fist pump my inner independent woman.

My prince isn't nearly as good at playing games as I am.

"How do you know Streven?" I ask my aunt in a low voice as Streven leans against the stair railing like he's been here a time or two. Or more. His gaze rakes across her curves, pausing on her lips before meeting her curious eyes.

"We're old friends." Her gaze holds too much warmth.

"Not that old." His tone rumbles with sensuality that makes me want to gag.

I step into my aunt's line of vision, cutting off the disturbing eye fucking that's happening right in front of me. "You have more important things to worry about than getting laid. We all do," I say the last part a little louder for the room to acknowledge.

Ryder rolls his eyes as he takes a seat on the petite couch. His legs spread wide, making him look too large for the small furniture.

"A lady never worries about such things." Lady Ivory's lips pull together, seemingly fighting off a smile.

"A lady just knows when such things are bound to happen." Her attention drifts to Streven and he gives her a cocky smile that makes me want to chuck a knife at his face all over again.

His bulky arms fold across his wide chest as he settles in against the glossy banister.

"It's true. You can't prevent destiny, Angel," Streven says.

Fury burns through me at the simple, taunting nickname.

Ryder pulls at my hand until I fall into his lap. The warmth of his palm pushes up and down my spine.

"Stop stressing. I swear your emotions have been crazy since you became a fae." I meld into him, resting my head against his shoulder. I'm exhausted and the war hasn't even begun yet. "When Darrio and Dax get here we need to be ready." He says it as if he's talking to no one in particular.

But I am. I'm happy and irritable and exhausted, but I'm completely ready for what's about to come.

Chapter Twelve

Short-Lived Happiness

It's late when the soldiers arrive. Darrio and Daxdyn step close to me, standing tall and proud before me. My fingers push absently back and forth across Nefarious' rough scales. It calms the creature as well as myself. He's sweeter than he seems. Friendly even.

The village is empty aside from a dozen mortals, armed with swords and sitting on their porches with nothing but mortal weapons and determination. Their gazes trail over the enormous crowd of fae warriors.

A tired silence clings to us. The rain has finally stopped, leaving behind a humid breeze that makes it hard to breathe.

"I sent a few dozen soldiers to the coast. Tristan will have a hard time managing the nix while they're feeding. It'll be at least a day before they make it across the sea." Darrio's eyes shift and I just know his mind is assessing every single detail of our situation. "I'm going to have Streven go down to the shore as well so he can shudder in and warn us if anything happens before tomorrow morning."

Tomorrow morning.

Our lives will be different then.

I step back from the dragon horse to address the waiting soldiers.

"In the morning we need to line the coast, barricade it with our magic to prevent them from entering at all." I don't want one single nix crawling over this land. These remaining mortals think they're brave. They have no idea what's coming.

My gaze shifts to the few mortals standing outside their homes. They stare up at me and the two fae men before me. There's awe within their eyes but also a hint of fear.

I can't do anything for that fear. They should be afraid. It is a very real terror that's about to hit this land.

"Take the night." I turn to our soldiers, my voice carrying over the crowd. The mass of them line the small, muddy streets, taking up every visible inch of this village. "Prepare your weapons; do not depend solely on your magic in the days to come." I pause, my gaze meeting theirs one by one. "The nix are not a match for us. We won't allow them to be. Their magic isn't blessed like ours is. We have *nothing* to fear." And we do not. It's all these mortals who are in real danger at the moment. Tristan's power is another story.

Nods of agreement follow my words. Darrio steps closer to me, a smile almost touching his serious features.

The small look warms me. It tingles right through me.

The deep voice of their commander booms through the streets.

"Until then, find a bed and make it your own. Try to get some rest." Darrio holds a careless stance.

Fearless. Never in my life have I found a word that completely describes someone. Until I met him.

Darrio turns to me, his stormy eyes searching my face.

He's entirely *fearless*.

***

The moon shines white through the windows, reminding me of the few hours of peace that we have here.

Streven is disgustingly sweet to my aunt. It almost makes me wish I liked him.

Almost.

He whispers words in her ear that makes her blush,

something I'm sure she hasn't done in over a decade.

Will they be this sickeningly cute after the war? Will the world change so much that he'd be willing to come here more often just to make my aunt smile like that?

I think hard and wonder if I've ever seen her this genuinely happy.

Her smile pulls to a frown as his body starts to fade away. When he's shuddered completely away her smile is gone entirely.

She drifts quietly through the room, her thoughts seeming far off in a forgotten time.

She slouches down on the couch next to me. Ryder sits with his thigh brushing mine on my other side.

"I was right." Her statement pulls at my attention and I cock a brow at her.

"You were right?"

A knowing little smirk tips her lips.

"Yes, I knew you four could be grinding harmony together."

Dax's lips part as he exchanges a sly glance with Ryder. Darrio rolls his eyes at the two of them before settling lazily in the arm chair across from me.

"You were absolutely right, Lady Ivory." Ryder gives

her a charming smile until I shove hard at his arm. His shoulder bumps mine and I try not to smirk at him.

"What will you all do after the war?" Her gaze skims around the room at the four of us.

After the war.

That thought hasn't crossed my mind at all.

Survival is all I've thought about really. I haven't ventured more than two days into the future of my messy thoughts.

"What do you mean?" Dax asks as he leans against the arm of the couch near Lady Ivory.

The crackling of the warm fire is the only sound for a few moments.

"Will the three of you still take care of my niece when the real world settles in? When society's judgmental gaze catches sight of your group relationship, will you still love her? Or is this just something to take your minds off of the reality that surrounds us?"

My stomach sinks at the honesty of her question.

Gods above, I hate how realistic her thoughts are right now.

Why haven't I asked myself these questions?

Have I been in denial with even myself?

If I am in denial, it's been a blissful little lie I've been living. Peaceful. Perfect even.

My life is perfect? I suppose it is perfect. It's the world that is imperfect.

Isn't it always?

"I've never really cared for society's thoughts." Darrio's deep voice startles me. "I think I speak for us all when I say I want to keep Kara any way she'll have me. Today and tomorrow. For as long as she'll put up with me." Darrio's gaze is fixated on the warm white color at the center of the fire. It reflects a look of intensity in his eyes that makes my breath catch.

He wants to keep me?

For a moment, silence passes the time as I keep my gaze locked on the sincere look in his eyes. Only the heavy pounding of my heart fills my thoughts.

"I'd hoped you'd say that." Lady Ivory's attention shifts to me with a small smile shining in her eyes. "I once had someone who cared for me every day of the week." Her hands clasp together in her lap and she focuses her attention there. "It's hard when realms rip you apart. In another life we could have been happy together. Never take happiness for granted. You don't know how quickly time changes. How quickly it passes."

The quietness in her voice strikes against my heart and I slip my hand over hers.

Sometimes I forget how much older than me she is. She doesn't look it, but she's lived years of loneliness. She's surrounded by a façade of love, but drowning in a reality of loneliness.

"I have some wine your father brought me for my birthday years ago." Her statement is so different it confuses me. "We should drink it. I've been saving it for a special occasion."

A beat passes and no one knows what to say.

No one but Dax it seems.

"And you think right now is a special occasion?"

My jaw clenches as my head turns slowly at his awful timing.

We've really got to talk about his empath abilities being canceled out by his awkward timing.

"Well, considering my niece is about to risk her life tomorrow, yes. Now or never is the perfect time." She stands and smiles at the four of us.

"You," she points at Ryder. "I like you. Follow me."

His brows raise and he looks at me.

"Should I be worried?" A smirk pulls at the corner of

his lips.

"You should be fucking terrified." It's a serious statement but it only makes him smile more. He brushes his palm down my arm before striding after my aunt into the other room. His steps are sure, and I may or may not watch him walk away for a bit too long.

Several minutes pass and dread starts to sink through my stomach.

Gods above I hope she's not giving him pointers on how to go down on me. Or worse, putting thoughts into his head. If she tries to tell him what a 'spit roast' is, I might die of mortification before the war even starts.

Dax's curiosity is pooling right into me as he listens intently to the whispering voices in the other room.

Ryder's wide smile sets me on edge when he returns. He takes his seat on the small couch, his thigh brushing against mine.

"What'd she say?" I hiss at him.

His arm slips against the back of the couch before wrapping warmly around me. He leans into me, his chest pushing against my shoulder as his lips skim over my ear.

"I'll tell you later." His breath against my neck sends a shiver down my back.

"Will you finish this off for me, Kara?" She places the

unopened bottle of wine on the table in front of me.

Finish it off for her? It's a whole bottle.

She's trying to get me relaxed. For whatever it is she just spoke to Ryder about.

My eyes narrow on her.

"Sure." Secretly, I'm still trying to figure out her angle.

Her gaze trails across my face.

"You haven't been happy in a long time. I want you to stay happy." Her voice drops soft and low. "I want you to stay this way forever." Her eyes, so similar to mine, shift across my wary smile.

I stand and quickly hug her before I lose the enthusiasm to show her affection.

"They love you," she whispers. "*I love you.*"

"I know." A pause drifts through my words. "I love you too." My voice sounds like an echo of hers.

Her palm pushes down my long hair just like my father used to do.

She squeezes tightly before pulling back to look at me.

She's always been like a sister to me. And in this peaceful moment I feel that now more than ever.

Her gaze shifts back to the men behind me as she starts to walk upstairs.

"Good night, Ryder." She winks at him in a secretive way that makes me spin on my heels.

Once she's out of sight, I storm back to him and he stands to meet my playful confrontation.

"What. Did. She. Say. To. You?"

His gaze darts to Dax's as his smile widens.

"I said I'd tell you later." His lips skim my jaw for only an instant.

A popping sound signals the cork coming out from the bottle. He starts to pour me a large glass of wine, but still all I can think about is the plethora of dirty knowledge my aunt has.

"Did she say something weird about a spit roast? Because she has a kind of weird personality, and I don't want whatever it is that she said to make things weird between us."

Daxdyn's laughter starts out quiet but the moment the other two men join him, it turns into this sound of happiness that makes me smile despite myself.

I shouldn't be this happy but I am. I actually don't remember the last time I was ever this happy.

"The words 'spit roast' never came up, I promise."
He kisses my lips slowly as he hands me the glass. I lean
into the affection as his palm settles low on my hip. It's
only a second. Just a brushing of our lips that steals my
breath away.

The red color stains the glass, and before I can even
hold it for longer than a second, Daxdyn's pulling the
much-needed drink away from me.

My brows pinch together. His lips part but he
doesn't say anything.

It's like he doesn't even know what to say. So we
only stare in confusion at one another for a moment.

He tips the glass to his lips and downs the whole
thing in a single drink.

"Wow, that—that was kind of rude." I take it back
from him and pour myself another as I try to ignore his
weird behavior.

I fill it to the rim and I can almost feel Daxdyn's
apprehension pushing into me. Once again, he steals the
drink away, sloshing a little over my knuckles before
downing it.

"Dax," I try to control the tremble of irrational anger
in my voice, "if you fucking touch this next glass of wine,
so help me gods—"

Fury shakes through me as he steals away the whole damn bottle and starts to chug.

"Stop being an asshole. You're supposed to be the sweet one! I don't know what your fucking problem's been lately, but I physically need that wine to sleep tonight."

He lowers the bottle and I stare up at his intense, stormy eyes. The aggression pushing against my chest reflects in his gaze. His emotions match mine in this instant and neither of us are budging.

My hands rise slightly and I don't think I've ever been this annoyed with anyone in my life.

In a single step, he crowds my body with his. His jaw tics as if there's something he wants to say but he refuses to open his mouth to let the words come out.

"Why are you being like this?" It's a small, uncontrollable shriek that's tearing at my voice.

"Because it's not good for our fucking baby," he yells back.

The breath in my lungs is forgotten. My lips part with a thousand unspoken words and all I can do is stare up at him and his fuming anger.

Protectively, my palm brushes over my flat stomach as fear begins to trickle in until it's flooding my body. My body that not even I understand apparently.

But this fae does.

I'm … pregnant?

The weird way he's been acting for the last few weeks skims through my mind. All the way back to when he asked me if I wanted kids when we stayed at his sister's house.

"You knew. You knew for weeks and you didn't tell me?" It's a quiet but rasping question that I have to force from my throat.

He fucking let me walk around here recklessly. He fucking watched me fight Druw. He fucking let me plan a war. He fucking knew and he didn't tell me.

The darkness in his gray eyes fades away. "Kara, I'm sorry." The gentle touch of his palm against my knuckles is shaken off.

"Don't touch me."

In a rush of angry steps, I push past him. Darrio sidesteps me, looking wide eyed. His gaze trails down my body, settling on my stomach for a long few seconds that make my emotions twist inside.

Until I shove past him as well.

And that's my problem; I've never needed anyone. I

don't know how to tell someone that I need them the most right now.

Chapter Thirteen

Ours

Every decision I've ever made flies through my mind as my stomach turns, threatening to vomit up every ounce of anxiety that's building within me.

"I just don't know," I whisper.

Ryder nods, his sky-blue eyes wide as he assesses the lavender colored curtains of the bedroom I've shut myself away in. He trailed in after me and didn't say a word. His presence is nice, but his silence is even nicer right now. He seems lost in a trance of his own fearful thoughts.

Is he as terrified as I am? Is he terrified of bringing the most innocent of life into this most awful world?

"I just ..." A heavy exhale leaves my lips. "I don't even know how this happened."

A line creases his brow and ever so slowly he pins me with a stunned look. The worry in his face turns to ridicule as he stares at me as if to ask if *Are you fucking serious right now*?

Every delicious, drawn out minute I've ever spent

with Ryder buried deep inside of me flashes through my mind, making me shift slightly with the memories.

All the times I've gotten caught up with Daxdyn and lost myself with Darrio skim through my thoughts on repeat.

"Okay, I know exactly how it happened." I roll my eyes at him before falling back on the bed. The mattress is soft beneath me. Without thinking, my palm settles over the smooth span of my stomach as if I'm attempting to protect the little life that's growing helplessly inside of me.

A mixture of worry and fear twirls through me as I study the texture of the white ceiling above.

The mattress dips, pulling me closer to Ryder as he takes a seat at the edge of the bed.

The warmth of his rough palm pushes slowly across my navel. My eyes meet his in an intensity of clashing emotions. A look of marvel is in his gaze, washing out the dreaded anxiety he previously held.

"Do …" He swallows hard as his thumb begins to skim back and forth against my skin. "Do you know whose it is?"

There's something intimate and exponentially extraordinary about the way he's looking at me.

He's scared. Just like me. He's not afraid of what our future holds, but what this child's future holds.

And I understand that entirely.

This beautiful fae baby will be perfect. Every part of it will be entirely perfect. But this world will take that perfection away.

So quickly.

And it scares the shit out of me.

I take a minute to consider the first time Dax and I had sex. And then Ryder. And then … both.

What the fuck is happening in my life for me to be this confused about every single thing?

"It's … not Darrio's." He can't have kids. I don't say it out loud. I might never.

I don't know why that strikes a piercing pain through my chest.

Darrio would be a good dad. Even if he pretends not to care about the topic at all. I know he does.

Ryder's large hand spans my abdomen as he skims his palm across my skin in a gentle way. His touch sends waves of tingles all through me.

I can't believe I was so careless. So reckless. There was just all this other stuff clouding over our lives recently, a child didn't cross my mind.

Until now.

"You know it doesn't matter, right?" He lies on his side, his body curling into mine as he holds me. Warm breath fans against my jaw as I let the worry that's tightening my chest consume me until I can't even breathe. "It doesn't matter, beautiful." His lips skim across my cheek. "We're a family. We always have been." For some reason, the comment pushes out some of the rising anxiety. "We're a family now. You're ours. This baby will be ours."

Again, his mouth skims against my cheek, pressing to the corner of my lips as a steady breath fills my lungs.

"You're ours. And so is this baby." He repeats in a quiet tone.

His head leans against mine as my eyes slowly close just as my throat tightens with too much emotion.

Because he's right. I know he is. It just feels nice to hear him say it.

I realize then, that I've never told him how much I love him. *I love him so much.* My lips part but I can't think of the perfect words.

Only a few moments pass when a gentle knock taps against the door. It's a quiet sound filled with uncertainty.

I know who it is before the door even opens.

Dax doesn't peek in or wait for my approval to enter. He steps in and shuts the door behind him. He leans against it, letting it support him as he stares down at me.

His attention is held on the way Ryder's hand is caressing my flat stomach.

"I'm sorry, Dax." My voice comes out weak and regretful.

I hate that I do everything wrong. I wish like hell I could treat him the way he treats me. But every time I start to get the hang of being a civilized girlfriend, the crazy in me sneaks back out before I can even stop it. I don't know why I'm like that.

It's a mystery, I tell you.

"Don't be sorry. I wanted to tell you. I just wanted you to tell me first, I guess. I wanted you to figure it out. You should know first, it's your body. I'm just the weird intrusive thing that knows everything about you before you even do." He's rambling. The disorderly locks of his hair fall into his tired eyes. It's then that I notice the darkness shadowing his eyes.

He's exhausted.

But he'll never show it. This beautiful man would die trying to make me happy.

"How do you feel?"

His question reminds me of every weird thing he's done over the last couple of weeks. He's been walking around, passing out caution signs for anyone that gets too close to me.

Maybe I'm not the only one who lets out the crazy sometimes.

"I'm fine." A warm feeling spreads through me as I sit up. Ryder's palm slips away from me. "Come here." It's a whispered demand that has him stalking toward me in an instant.

My hands settle around his lean hips and his fingers skim down the length of my arms.

"Lie down."

An unsure smile tilts his lips.

"Really? Right now?" His gaze drifts to Ryder as if he's calculating the setting.

Sex. He's thinking about sex right now.

"I think you should sleep, Dax." Laughter shakes through me. Sleep was the furthest thing from his mind, I swear it.

His fingers thread through my hair, caressing but controlling, and suddenly I don't care at all if he sleeps. His gaze holds mine as he bends closer to me. A shaking breath is held in my lungs as he presses his lips to my temple before flopping down at my side.

I jostle a little, thrown off balance by the switch in his emotions and the weight of his body.

We were almost all on the same page.

Damn it.

Daxdyn's long lashes fall closed as he pushes his hands beneath his head. His dark shirt rides up slightly, revealing the hard panes of his abdomen. For once, he looks peaceful, youthful and, of course, beautiful.

I peek over at Ryder to find him smirking at his friend.

The three of us lie like that, horizontal on the little twin bed meant for one. Our legs hang off the side and it shouldn't be the most comfortable position, but with them surrounding me it is. I'm more relaxed than ever between them.

I'm faintly aware of Ryder standing to turn off the light. The bed dips once more and his warmth is right there in place again at my side.

My lashes fall heavily closed just as he speaks.

"We should … wake him up."

My eyes barely open, already prepared for sleep.

Ryder's wide awake, staring at me intently.

"What?" I mumble.

He turns to me, his palm skimming my neck. His warm touch pushes down my collarbone, pushing down my chest before he rubs his thumb back and forth against my nipple.

"I said, you should wake him up." His lips brush against the column of my throat slowly.

My lashes flutter closed with a heavy breath.

"I think he needs sleep."

His head dips and his teeth rake across my nipple through my thin shirt and a quiet gasp tears from my lips.

"If that's what you want." Warm palms push against my shirt until his tongue is sweeping across my stomach. The bed shifts as he kisses a path down my torso.

"Do whatever you want, but I'm sleeping, Ryder." It's a breathy statement that doesn't hold much conviction, but I cling to that careless demeanor.

"Mmm, you're probably going to have the sweetest dreams." His breath fans against my navel as he jerks my jeans down my hips. He shoves them down my legs. I do my best not to help him, to try to pretend I have no interest in what he's doing.

I try, really I do.

Until I kick hastily at the clothing preventing his hands from being on my body.

My boots and jeans land on the hardwood floor with a quiet thud.

I don't open my eyes. It causes a swirling sense of anticipation to build in my chest as I listen to him shift from the bed.

Big palms push up my thighs. The feel of his hands on my hips sends a shiver all through me.

Warm kisses skim over the inside of my thigh. I spread my legs for him wider.

With strong hands, he grips my hips and jerks me closer to the edge of the bed. A small gasp shakes across my lips.

My heart pounds just waiting.

Nothing's even happened and my nerves are strumming all through my body.

A breath kisses my skin, right where I want him.

My leg bends as he places my foot on his shoulder.

His palms settle beneath my ass, gripping me tightly.

Soft lips press over my entrance in a torturously slow movement. I almost moan with need.

He's trying to kill me, I know it.

This is what I get for saying I'd rather sleep.

Finally, the flat of his tongue parts my folds. With one long stroke he licks up before swirling his tongue hard against my clit.

He groans against me, humming his pleasure over my sex. His tongue slips in, filling me and making me gasp for air.

Deeper he delves in before bringing his mouth back up. He sucks hard against my clit until I cry out. My hips grind shamelessly against him and he holds me tightly in place. His nails sink into my skin as he sucks before rolling his wide tongue caressingly against me. The alternating sensation has the energy in my core bundling so tightly I can't even think.

Soft hair meets my fingertips and I fist it in both hands, holding him to me.

His tongue rolls up my sex once more. His teeth rake lightly across my clit before sucking and I come against the caressing pain of it all.

My moan is a crying sound that only becomes more

ragged as he strokes his tongue against my shaking orgasm. He laps it up, almost licking harder the more I cry out.

When he finally pulls back from me, the tension leaves my body, leaving me weak for several seconds.

"Wake him up."

I blink hard at the darkness of the room. The features of Ryder's face are shadowed but the white moonlight hits his hooded eyes in shining colors.

I turn, wanting to think of something sexy to say to wake Daxdyn up, but his lips meet mine in the dark. Daxdyn kisses me firmly. His strong hands pull at my hips until I'm settled over him.

His lean hips are beneath me and before I lower myself, his hand is between my legs. Long fingers stroke against my slickness.

A rumbling groan shakes through his chest as he takes his time running his index finger up and down my sex. His palm is wet from my orgasm and he rubs hard at my clit until I'm gasping against his lips.

"You're not a very quiet sleeper," Dax whispers.

I try to think of a witty response through my hazy mind but my words die on my lips as Ryder's palm pushes down the curve of my ass. His fingers meet

Daxdyn's, slipping against my wetness before pulling back up. His index finger circles my ass slowly and my spine stiffens.

"Has—anyone ever fucked you here?" His breath is warm against my neck, sending a shiver across my skin.

Daxdyn's fingers sink into me, pushing deeper as I try to think about Ryder's question.

"Yes," I breathe out the response and shift against Daxdyn's hand.

His pace quickens. The heel of his palm grinds against my clit as he pounds into me.

"Did you like it?" Ryder's fingers tease my ass and I arch against his touch.

"No." Simple one-word answers are all I have.

Ryder's lips press to the base of my neck, his tongue sweeping warmly across my skin.

"Maybe he did it wrong." His whisper makes me smile even as Daxdyn starts to kiss me slowly.

They're so good at distracting me. They're a small team of sexy distraction.

Ryder's index finger sinks very slowly in and I do rock against their palms at the feel of being filled.

I consider how big Ryder is and it's a hard no. It's not

going to happen. I pull back from Dax just slightly.

"There is another option for the three of us." I have their attention as they both pause to listen to what I might say next.

"Whatever you want. Tell me what you want." Dax waits patiently but neither of them stop the slow stroking that's pulling a quiet moan from my lips. On a shaking exhale I consider my words.

Ryder listens intently. A smirk tilts at my mouth as I start to speak.

"You could always fuck Dax while I watch."

Every muscle in their bodies halt. No one moves an inch. All sexy assaults on my body have come to a complete stand still.

"That—that doesn't sound like a good time at all, Kara." Dax even pulls back from me slightly.

"No, that's—that's not an option." Ryder's voice is more serious than I've ever heard it.

My head tips back to look at his pretty blue eyes.

"Then maybe you should get your hand out of my ass and *share*."

Ryder would never make me do something I didn't want to. I know that. But the awkward look in his eyes right now is priceless.

"I'm sorry. Your aunt said all this shit. She made me feel like I didn't even know what sex was. Fucking talking about groundhogs and French third base. I have no idea what yab yum means and she said it like three times." His words are a stream of worry and it makes me smile from the anxiety my aunt must have gave him.

I told him he should have been afraid.

He exhales a heavy breath.

"I'm sorry. You know I want to make you happy. Tell me what you want me to do." He leans in to me, his lips kissing my bottom lip sweetly before kissing me fully.

"Lie down," I say in a quiet voice.

He looks lost. His gaze shifts from me to Dax. Slowly, he pulls away from me and climbs up to the pillow. Dax sits up to the edge of the bed, still holding me while Ryder rests behind him. Once more, Ryder's attention settles on me.

"Take your shirt off." He smirks as if it's adorable that I'm telling him what to do, but he does it. His hands grip the back of his shirt as he pulls it off. The hard lines of his arms flex as he tosses the shirt to the floor.

"Lie back."

Tension consumes his movements as he hesitantly

lies against the fluffy pillow. It's as if he's waiting for a surprise attack instead of sex.

My palms run down the corded muscles of Daxdyn's arms. The smooth feel of his body makes me want more.

Hard panes meet my fingertips as I push up his abdomen. Warm breaths become heavier against my neck while I rub my palms against his pecs. He releases me slowly, helping me pull off his soft shirt. I toss it to the floor with Ryder's.

For a second, I just take them in. They're sexy together. Shirtless and strong and waiting.

Just for me.

But they only wait so long.

Ryder's fingers unfasten his jeans. He holds my gaze as he shoves them down his hips. The sight of his hard dick makes me shift against Daxdyn's chest.

I stand to step back from them both, standing between Dax's spread legs.

Ryder's heated gaze follows my every move. My bare thighs rub together and I slowly pull at the hem of my white shirt. My fingertips skim against my navel as I bring it over my head.

I'm naked before them.

Daxdyn leans back, his arms brushing against Ryder as he gets comfortable watching me.

I've never felt as wanted as I do right now. It's a tingling feeling that starts in my core but trembles through my heart as well.

I keep my eyes on Ryder as I lean into Dax and kiss him deeply. As Ryder's palm wraps around his cock my eyes flutter closed, tangling my tongue with Daxdyn's.

As my tongue rolls against his, my hand trails down the lines of his hard chest. His hips shift when my fingers quietly unbutton his jeans.

My fingers skim down his throbbing length and his breath catches against my lips. His light touch feels hesitant against my skin as his fingertips trail over my ribs before palming my breast. I arch into the bruising pressure of his kiss. His thumb brushes against my nipple as his palm pushes firmly against my breast.

An ache courses through me, demanding more. I take a step back but never release him. He leans into me, keeping our lips locked. My wrist continues rolling up and down slowly against his shaft and he groans against my lips before following after me.

Slow steps bring us to the foot of the bed. His tongue rolls leisurely against mine and when I back up against the mattress I finally pull my hand away. A minimal amount of space separates us as he leans back to look me in the eye.

His hooded gaze is smoky and filled with swirling magic that might always take my breath away. My fingers drift against his palm lightly. I keep my eyes on his as I turn and crawl up the bed on all fours. My hands rest against Ryder's hips, my fingers etching the lines veering down to the cock he's stroking slowly.

I look back at Daxdyn just before I lower my head. He watches me intently. A whirling feeling of anticipation consumes my core as my lips press to the tip of Ryder's cock. My legs are spread intentionally. My spine is arching toward the mattress, giving Daxdyn what I know must be an inviting sight.

As my tongue swirls over the top of Ryder's head, his eyes fall closed, his palm brushing over my knuckles as my hand wraps slowly around his thickness.

I study him in this moment. Taking in his relaxed and beautiful features. His head tips slightly back, giving me the angle of his strong jaw. A deep breath parts his lips just as my mouth wraps fully around his dick.

The taste of him fills my mouth and I take him as far as I can, sucking hard and feeling his tip hit the back of my throat. A low groan hums through his chest.

The mattress dips and more energy tingles through

me as I wait with wanting nerves spiraling through me.

Daxdyn's fingers grip my hips slowly, one finger after the other. My eyelids flutter and it urges me on with faster movements against Ryder until he fists my hair in his hands. He pulls lightly as he guides my quick pace against his cock.

"Fuck, Kara." Ryder's voice is a rasping sound that strums through my core.

Daxdyn's hand runs over the curve of my ass. Slowly, his fingers push against my sex, palming me in his hand. I shift shamelessly against his touch.

But he's gone as quickly as he came. Cool air skims over my body where his hands once were. I almost pout against Ryder's cock.

Yes, everyone pity the poor woman with not enough dicks filling her.

Seriously, what is he doing—

He slams into me so hard my moan hums against Ryder's dick and an unrepressed groan with a hint of shaking laughter reverberates through Ryder's chest.

With long, powerful strokes, he thrusts into me, filling me so deep I tremble in his hands. He holds tightly to my hips. Closer he shifts toward me until his knees are planted beneath me as he rocks deeper into me.

It's a steady and demanding pace.

In only a few moments, Daxdyn's quick thrusting causes my orgasm to shake through me until I can't even focus on Ryder, but neither men seem to notice my lack of concentration.

Ryder's hips rock beneath my palms and his fingers tighten in my hair as he guides his cock deeper into my mouth.

I'm shaking between them. The energy in me builds, making my spine arch into Ryder's body. He releases his tight hold on me and I pull back, my palm wrapping fully around his length. My breath shakes as another orgasm tightens within me. Daxdyn groans from behind me. It's a violent sound, like he's losing control but is trying to hold on just for me.

I feel my walls tighten around his hard dick and as I start to tremble in their hands, Daxdyn finally stills behind me with a low groan.

Waves pulse through me. I'm gripping Ryder's dick but his pleasure is long forgotten.

I almost feel bad for him.

Until he speaks.

"Lie down." His rumbling words echo mine.

It's what I said to him not long ago, but the heat in

his gaze makes me shift against Daxdyn's dick that's still pulsing hard within me.

Daxdyn's palm brushes slowly over my ass before he slips himself from me.

A hollow feeling settles in but I know it won't be there long.

Ryder's fingers push up the inside of my arm and he pulls lightly until I settle in, lying comfortably with my back against his pillow.

How many orgasms is one person capable of having?

His tongue rolls across his lower lip and I suddenly really want to find out.

The mattress shifts as Ryder's hard body covers mine.

Daxdyn watches our every move as he settles in against the foot of the bed. His jeans are slung low against his slim hips, but his boxers cover up his impressive erection.

Warm lips skim against my jaw and the slick head of Ryder's dick teases my sensitive clit.

He groans as his teeth rake across my neck. Lowering his head, his lips move until his breath fans against the curve of my shoulder. He kisses there gently before sinking his teeth in hard enough to make me gasp. His tongue sweeps quickly over my skin just as he pushes slowly into me.

My fingers dig into his strong arms that are strung tight beneath my touch.

His weight is held carefully above me as our hips rock in perfect rhythm. His gaze trails my features as he sinks into me over and over again. He takes his time. It doesn't feel like it did the first time. It isn't rushed and hard.

It's slow and consuming.

I try to hold his gaze. I try to let him see that I'm hanging on by a thread but my eyes roll, my head tipping back as he takes his time fucking me. His lips meet the column of my exposed throat, and he kisses me there as I hold on to him tightly by his shoulders. Sweat dampens his skin and still he takes his time.

I can't take it.

My palms meet his taut shoulders and I push at him until he understands. His fingers dig into the underside of my thighs, locking me in place against him. In one swift move he rolls us. I'm poised perfectly on top of him. His dick is still deep within me.

In life, Ryder is well thought out, putting all of his effort into what he does.

Sex with Ryder is no different.

I like it. I like looking down on that sated look in his eyes. I especially like the way his jaw tenses with the slowest grinding of my hips.

The mattress shifts, dipping low around us.

Rough palms push against my hips, carefully and lightly skimming.

I pause. My hair catches against my lip, my breath fanning heavily as I lock eyes with Darrio. Iron eyes study me, trailing every feature. My movements halt entirely. I'm unsure of myself suddenly. Unsure of us in a way.

Daxdyn is nowhere to be seen. It's as if he slipped out while I wasn't looking. *Did he leave to make Darrio more comfortable?*

My heart pounds wildly as we stare at one another.

Darrio's legs straddle over Ryder's as he leans closer to me. His chest is bare, revealing slashing scars and strong lines. The buckle of his jeans is low and undone.

Warm breath fans over my shoulder as he slowly presses his lips there. The smooth panes of his chest against my body, and my chest against Ryder's sends a tingling and knowing feeling all through me. His hips rock against the curve of my ass.

The two men make it hard to think but I do try to find words.

"Ac—actually we discussed this and that's not going to happen." Uneven tones catch at my words as I try to think clearly. "None of you guys are fun size and I rather like my asshole just the way it is."

Darrio's eyes close and he almost shakes his head at me. The smallest of smiles tugs at his lips.

"Just relax." His light touch pushes down the length of my spine, making my hips shift against Ryder's dick.

Agonizingly slow movements brush against my back, distracting me and taunting me all at the same time. His palm pushes down the curve of my ass making me tense beneath his touch.

Ryder holds my gaze before leaning forward and sealing his lips to mine. Rolling flicks of his tongue have my eyes fluttering closed.

When Darrio's fingers sink slowly into me, sliding up the length of Ryder's dick, my mouth parts with a shaking moan. It brings a new and reckless feeling trembling through me.

But he's gone as quickly as he came.

Ryder's warm palms skim up my ribs, caressing the weight of my breasts. It takes all my concentration to focus on just Ryder and not the both of them. When Darrio's dick runs smooth against my inner thigh I tense once more against Ryder.

I want Darrio here. I do. More than anything. But I don't think this is going to work.

Just as I pull back from Ryder, Darrio's dick slides against me. It's slick against my sex and against Ryder's shaft. Ryder's brows raise slightly, his palms becoming still against my body.

Suddenly, he looks more nervous than I am. This is new for all of us. And too much thinking will make it all fall apart.

My fingers grip Ryder's jaw and I pull him back to my mouth, pulling him under with the distraction of my lips.

A thundering sound consumes my heart as Darrio starts to sink in inch by inch. It's a slow and unhurried process. The stiff feel of Ryder's shoulder relaxes and a rumbling groan shakes through his chest.

Filled and Fucked. All I can think of is how fantastically filled and fucked I am right now.

The two of them fill me completely, pushing hard at just the right angles. Darrio's grip on my hip tightens and his nails sink into my skin as he slowly rocks his length into me. Ryder's palms push down my body and he holds me in place. I'm between the hard panes of their chests but a consuming current is building within my core.

Ryder's lips brush over my jaw line. He sucks lightly against my neck. His groans are low and humming over my skin.

I've never been this wet and I've never felt this turned on in my entire life. I haven't ever had men in my life that wanted me like these men want me.

"Darrio … " My nails rake down Ryder's shoulders. I cling to him and he lets me. He supports me entirely.

At the sound of his name, Darrio's slow stroking becomes a bit quicker. The head of his cock grinds against Ryder's length as he slams into me hard over and over again.

My orgasm shakes through me so hard I tremble between their arms. Darrio holds on to me tighter and Ryder holds me more firmly in place. Rumbling sounds of their pleasure hum through the room as my sex tightens against their cocks.

"Fuck," Ryder's head tips back and I know the moment he comes. I see it in the tightness of his jaw and I feel it as Darrio slides into me once more.

Darrio's palms squeeze my waist hard and a moment later he stills against my body.

All that can be heard is our harsh and gasping breaths.

Very carefully, Darrio slips himself from me. His bruising grip becomes a caressing touch as he pulls back from me.

Ryder's lips skim my neck in a sweet kiss. His eyes hold mine in a hooded way as I start to pull back. My hips lift from his, a soreness clings to my limbs. I take a quiet seat against the wall, my legs thrown across Ryder's lap. It takes a second for me to have the nerve to meet Darrio's smoky gaze.

Reality falls into place fast. It crashes down on us.

"Was that ... weird?" My fingers start to pick at the white thread of the tangled quilt.

Darrio leans back, still kneeling as he was before.

"It was—really tight."

"Really fucking *tight*," Ryder says with more, and slightly better emphasis.

Tight. Yes, that's good, right? Any other descriptions?

The door opens and Daxdyn slips inside quickly. A knowing smirk tilts his lips. His attention drifts between myself and his brother but he doesn't speak. Quietly he takes a seat at the edge of the bed. His palm pushes back and forth against my ankle like he just wants to touch me. To reassure me.

"You liked it?" I peek at Ryder's completely content features for only a second before I realize he's definitely not the one I have to worry about here.

My gaze drifts back to Darrio.

He studies every part of me. His attention burns across my damp skin. Slowly his fingers slip through mine.

"Honestly, I didn't think I would. But …"

He pauses at the most inconvenient time.

"But?" I urge him on to tell me every insignificant thought in his head right now.

His mouth opens but no words come out.

"Would you do it again?" I'm trying. I'm trying so hard to make sure this wasn't a relationship ruining mistake.

Amazing sex isn't worth the cost of my relationship with them.

So, when his lips part I'm clinging to the words he hasn't even spoken yet.

And they surprise the hell out of me.

"I'd do it again in a fucking heartbeat."

A smile parts my lips as I stare up at Darrio.

These beautiful men push their limits for me. And they'd do it again in a fucking heartbeat.

"I think this only works if we're honest and open." Ryder's gaze darts away from mine, as he studies the tangled blanket on the bed.

Daxdyn's serious attention falls hard on his friend. The empath's emotions change from light to heavy in an instant and it sinks right into me.

What is Ryder thinking?

"You're right," I whisper, trying to ignore the quiet but demanding feeling of Daxdyn's emotions. He's not going to talk about it. Not right now anyway. "And honestly, I'm exhausted. So ... who's going to clean me up?"

Darrio smirks down at me, his lips pressing against the curve of my jaw.

"Some things you have to do yourself, human." He pulls back from me, giving me one more quick kiss against the corner of my lips before shoving away from me and the clean-up I just suggested.

Daxdyn also strides away. I look to Ryder and he shakes his head slowly at me.

"Have you ever heard the phrase *lie in the mess*

you've made. That's all you." He winks at me before leaping from the bed and striding after his friends.

I'll be lucky if I can stand without falling after all of that.

What a bunch of rude assholes.

A line creases my brow as I dwell on how much more appealing this was an hour ago.

The door creaks open once more and the three of them come right back to me.

Darrio crawls up the bed in a predatory way. My lips part as his mouth covers mine. His rumbling words hum against my lips.

"We wouldn't love and leave you."

"We're not that big of dicks." Ryder's smirk matches Daxdyn's and his fingers lace with mine.

I'm astounded by their sweetness. I'm even more astounded they let a big dick joke go to waste.

Sometimes they're perfect.

Sometimes.

Chapter Fourteen

Don't Ever Worry

The pelting sound of rain striking against the house wakes me just as thunder rumbles, shaking all through Saint's Inn.

My lashes flutter open to find Ryder's pale eyes watching me. The four of us lie on the hard floor, piled together uncomfortably just to be near one another. Darrio lies between my legs, sprawled over me with his big arms wrapped around my small frame. He holds me like he wants to be a little closer to our baby.

Our baby.

The words hum through my mind, and as if he can sense my mixture of happiness and anxiety, Daxdyn slips his arm across my shoulders, melding his body closer to my side.

I love the way he knows me inside and out. Daxdyn's gift isn't the strongest power I've ever seen, but it fits him so perfectly. I can't imagine him any other way.

Lightning flashes through the room, lighting up every dark crevice. It strikes through Ryder's serious eyes in a way that makes my stomach uneasy. He leans closer, his head resting on our shared pillow. Our noses nearly touch from our closeness.

A heavy pause fills the silence just before he presses his lips to mine. His lips silence whatever it is that's drifting through his head. His tongue parts my mouth as he kisses me hard. He stops the kiss, but then his mouth is on mine again. Slow kisses press to my lips, tightening a feeling deep within me with every skimming flick of his tongue. There's another slow pause as he pulls back slightly, as if he's not sure if he should.

The back and forth has me panting and confused all at once.

Hesitantly, he rolls his tongue against mine. His lips seal to my own before he pulls back once more. His eyes hold mine as our breaths clash against each other.

"I love you." It's a rumbling and whispered confession that makes his eyes close. It makes him look like he wants to disappear from here. And yet, he holds me tighter as if *I* might disappear from here.

His words make my breath catch in my throat, my eyes widening as I stare up at this beautiful man.

"I love you too." Sincerity and emotion flood my words.

"I—I loved you before." He clears his throat, meeting my gaze with a hooded look that sinks right through me. "I loved you before we had sex. I loved you before we ever stepped foot into the Hopeless realm. I loved you the moment we danced. I held you close in front of that whole fucking room of pretentious people in the castle I grew up in, knowing I couldn't have you." His words shake through his chest, feeling unsteady against my heart. "And now I do. I have you and I'm *terrified* of losing you." He swallows at the sound of the emotion that's building in his chest.

"What do you mean *lose me*, Ryder?"

A frightening feeling begins to eat away at the fluttering sensation his sweet words just gave me.

I know what he's about to say before he says it. I've just carefully avoided the truth for so long I'm not even sure I want to know now.

"In the Traveler's Guild, when the gods gave me a vision of the future," my heart pounds hard, threatening to roar over the sound of his wavering voice, "Darrio saves you." His brows crease as he says his friend's name and, for a moment, confusion floods me.

"Are you worried he might not? That he might not get to me in time?"

His teeth sink into his lower lip as his eyes close slowly again.

"He dies saving you, Kara."

Those words slam into me. My hands drop from his warm body and I swear my heart stops beating all together.

My heart refuses to beat if Darrio Riles isn't there to hear it.

***

I want to sleep. I want to rest before tomorrow comes. Not just because of the war that's looming, but because I have to protect him. I have to protect all of them.

But all I can think about is how sweet Darrio feels wrapped around me. How warm and comforting this man is in my arms.

My fingers push through his long hair. Darrio's strong. Unyielding. Shit, he's downright terrifying.

Could Tristan really take him away from me?

My throat is tight as I swallow hard against that thought.

I tilt my head to find Ryder finally asleep. His lips are parted as even breaths fan across my neck.

I turn and Daxdyn's smooth features are relaxed. Calm and serene.

Darrio's head is turned into my body, resting against

my stomach as his heavy sighs skim across my abdomen.

I shift between all of them. It takes effort, but I slip from beneath Darrio's body and Daxdyn and Ryder's arms. I tug my jeans on as quietly as possible. My arms shove into my shirt as I open the door.

My steps are unsteady, my legs feeling weak beneath me.

I need a real plan. I need space to think. And I can't do that when Darrio's death looms in my mind every time I look at his handsome face.

Darkness surrounds me as I make my way into the dimly lit living room. Flickering light dance across the shadows along the wall.

And there seated before the small fire, is a woman whose face doesn't possess a single wrinkle despite the worry held in her eyes.

"Why aren't you asleep?" I hiss at my aunt.

Her head tilts as she pins me with a mocking stare.

"I tried but there was this incredibly loud fuck fest that kept interrupting my sweet and innocent dreams."

I cock a brow at her, my hip jutting out slightly.

"You did not hear us."

Her lips part with an incredulous smile.

"I heard the encore loud and clear, darling."

My eyes close slowly as I make my way over to her and take a seat at her side. The fire warms my face. It's peaceful tonight.

"You didn't have to fill Ryder's head with all that French third base stuff."

Her thin lips tip up in a sultry smile.

"The thoughts were already there, Kara. I just shoved the thoughts into actions."

"He knows how to use his dick without your fantastic help." My head shakes slowly and I try hard not to think about what Ryder said to me less than an hour ago. I'd much rather talk about this.

"Your face is a little sour for someone who just had sex with three beautiful fae men. Unappreciative little thing, aren't you?" Her boney elbow knocks into mine and I roll my eyes at her despite the smile that's threatening my lips.

"I—I'm afraid for them." My voice is a quiet sound that teeters with too much pent-up emotions. "It's hard worrying about one person. How will I ever survive worrying about three?"

Four. I have to remind myself that soon, there will be another for me to worry over.

My fingers tap lightly against my abdomen in thought. Lady Ivory's thin arms wrap around me as a heavy breath shakes from my lungs.

"You've only ever had to worry about yourself, Kara." Her head leans against mine as her quiet voice sinks into me. "But you never noticed there were people worrying about you."

My stomach dips as I realize she's worried about me for years.

And never once did I worry about her.

She's strong and resilient.

I never had to worry about her.

But she's always worried about me.

"No matter how capable someone is, we will always think about them. But stress does nothing for the mind." She squeezes my shoulder hard and I lean into her. She's been the only family I have had for so long that I've started to take her for granted. I didn't stop in to see her enough. I didn't ever tell her how much I appreciated her. I didn't tell her I loved her often enough. "Don't worry. Do not ever worry. Take action instead. Find strength in your stresses and use it to change all the things that dwell in your mind. But do not ever waste time worrying about what you know you have the strength to change."

My heart beats louder as I start to nod.

She's right. She's always so smart. She knows just the right thing to say.

I won't worry about the future.

I'll change it.

Chapter Fifteen

An Awful Plan

I wake to the startling sound of boots storming through the house. I shove up from my spot on the tiny couch. A sharp pain shoots through my neck and I wince from the uncomfortable feel of it.

My gaze drifts through the living room, finding it empty.

I fell asleep here. But my aunt no longer sits at my side.

I shove off from the couch and start pushing my feet into my boots as I follow the echoing sound of endless footsteps. My thighs tense in pain with every step I take.

Perhaps fantastic sex before war wasn't my brightest idea.

But I'd be lying if I said I wouldn't choose the amazing mistake all over again.

Darrio's hair is tied tightly back as he listens to Ryder speak in quiet tones. My lips part at the sight of him. My heart aches as if he'll be ripped away from me at any moment.

Soldiers come in and out to speak with one another before racing out once again through the back door. I begin buckling my belt, securing my blade at my side.

Daxdyn walks toward me. The three of them are dressed in clothes of black leather. My fingers reach out to skim over the smooth material that's sturdy beneath my touch. The inky color catches the sunlight, glittering oddly against the rays.

"It's dragon's leather. Strong but beautiful."

My gaze meets Daxdyn's iron-like eyes, his sharp features and the hint of a perfect smile on his lips.

Strong but beautiful.

"I had the guys dig one up for you too." Daxdyn reaches behind him and grabs a cloth of glistening leather for me as well.

It isn't armor. It's more like another layer of clothing. But magic glistens over every dark scale.

Is it protected somehow?

It's soft against my hands. Daxdyn keeps his close proximity with me, his fingers drifting down to rest on my hip.

"I—I heard what Ryder said last night." His words are spoken quietly, and even though I hear him, I don't look up. I keep my attention held on the dragon's

166

leather in my palms. "Everything's going to be alright, Kara." He leans in to press his lips to my temple but I tip my head up at the last minute. On the toes of my boots, I lean into him. His lips land lightly against mine, and I close my eyes at the calming feel of it.

Daxdyn was the first. Darrio might have been the first man I ever loved, but Daxdyn was my first real friend. He made me laugh when I thought happiness wasn't real. He urged me to be more than just a simple human. He saved me when I thought I was dying.

Our friendship makes us stronger. And that's how I know he's the only person I can say this to.

We keep close together. His chest pushes against mine as our hair brushes slightly together. My fingers lace through his and I hold his deep and knowing gaze.

"If it comes down to him or me," I pause, choosing my whispered words carefully. "Don't hesitate to save him. Say you'll keep him safe."

The starry color of his eyes narrows on me. Everyone around us continues on. But only he and I are in this moment.

"You're carrying our baby, Kara. And even if you weren't, I'd never promise you something like that."

"I'm not asking you to promise. A promise is an insignificant thing. Not reliable at all really. Nothing but words and whispers." My voice cracks as I try to keep a quiet tone. "I'm asking for action. I'm asking you to choose your brother over me if you have to. I was only a thief when we first met. The world will not miss a thief."

His gaze shifts calculatingly over my features.

"I *promise*. I promise I'll save him over you."

His words circle my mind.

They're pointed and sharply spoken as if he has no intentions of doing that at all.

He promises.

What a dick.

A smile tilts my lips.

What a smart and taunting asshole.

"I love you," my voice shakes slightly. "Never promise me anything."

His lips brush lightly over mine.

"I *promise*, I won't."

Those simple words make my heart flutter.

They almost make me forget the world for a few short minutes.

He pauses there, holding on to me for just a

moment longer.

Ryder and Darrio both look to the two of us. I feel their gazes but I'm not ready to abandon the safe feel of his arms.

I pull back from him slowly.

It takes a second for me to find a sense of normalcy between the swirling calm and the fighting anxiety within me.

"Where's Streven? He hasn't come to warn us? Tristan really hasn't crossed the sea yet?"

Darrio shakes his head slowly at me.

The sun is just beginning to creep onto the horizon, casting a hazy hue against the warm morning air. A table separates us, the glossy surface reflects the bright sunlight.

"Tristan's plotting something." I pause as I consider it. "He wants us to come to him. He wants to draw us away from these villages."

"You really think he's that smart?" Dax looks to me as my mind reels with the possibilities.

I begin pulling the dragon leathers over my head like a tee shirt. It's tight, but I force it down. When I pull my hair back, the three men are all zeroed in on my chest. My shirt's pulled down and the vest-like leather is thinner than expected. It presses snugly against my breasts, pushing hard against them until they're amplified and—honestly—fantastic.

"Are they bigger?" My brows pull together as I look at myself just like the men are looking at me.

"Definitely." Ryder's voice is full of awe and appreciation. He's all but clapping with gratitude.

"The enemy's going to be really distracted when they see you." Daxdyn still doesn't meet my gaze and I have to shove his shoulder hard to get him to find my narrowed eyes.

"Sorry," he says, looking quickly away.

"Anyway," I breathe out a sigh. "We can't go after him."

My teeth sink into my lower lip as I consider our predicament.

"We could always smoke him out." Darrio's cocky gaze meets mine.

"The city's already on fire. If he hasn't been smoked out in the last twenty years, I doubt it'll happen now."

The visions the Travelers gave me flicker through my mind. I didn't encounter Tristan until nightfall. We were losing when I did. The nix were ripping through this realm like they would devour it whole in less than an hour.

And yet here we wait.

"We need to find him. We need to draw him out."

"Going there without our army is suicide." Darrio's voice interrupts my thoughts, reminding me of what Ryder told me just hours ago.

"You're right. You should stay with our soldiers." Stay here. Away from me and away from the danger. "Ryder and I will find him. We'll taunt him and we'll bring him here on our terms."

"That sounds like an awful plan. Dax and I should at least go with you." Darrio's hard gaze holds mine, waiting for me to relent.

My head tilts to the side, in a challenging way.

"Show of hands who thinks Darrio should follow me to attack Tristan?" I don't even look away as I wait for the show of hands that I know will not raise.

Darrio's lips thin as he looks to Daxdyn and then to Ryder.

"Perfect," a smile perches on my lips, "let's go, Ryder."

I can't bring myself to look at him as I stride out the door, pushing past a soldier on my way.

Ryder's boots stomp after me and I don't pause for him to catch up.

"You know this is a shitty idea, right?"

He protests, but he also knows my reasons.

"Do you have a better idea?"

His silence makes my heart thunder to life with anxiety and adrenaline.

"Ready?" I ask.

"Shouldn't I be asking you that?"

"Nope. For once you get to know what it feels like."

"Know what *what* feels like?"

A smile tilts my lips as I grip his forearm. Realization crosses his features just before I tear us away.

It feels good to give him a taste of his own medicine.

So good that my smile is plastered wide across my face when we land. He stumbles out of my grip, barely righting himself just before his face meets the muddy shore.

"Yeah, that feels like shit." He coughs hard like he can't catch his breath and it only makes my smile grow impossibly larger.

Cold water laps against my boots and the sky looks

stormier here. The smoke overtakes the heavens, clouding them with pollution. It's darker here and I start to wonder if I really met Tristan at nightfall or if the sky was just overrun with the darkness of the smoke.

Ryder's fingers skim down the inside of my wrist.

"Should we start at the castle?" He looks out into the heart of the smoky city.

An eerie silence lingers in the air. No mortals or creatures are seen. Everything is unnaturally quiet.

"No."

"No?"

The hair on my arms stand as a crawling feeling creeps down my spine.

"No, they're here."

The gray foam of the sea clings to my boots and my gaze follows the waves out, trailing carefully over the ocean.

White eyes blink back at me. My gaze strains to focus on the white among the dark sea. Slick blue skulls bob within the deep waves. Thousands of them dot the ocean, peppering it with ominous creatures who watch our every move.

Dread drags through my chest as I start to speak.

"I take it back, let's get to the castle."

In a flash, Ryder's magic mingles with mine, ripping me away from the dangerous shores of Juvar.

Chapter Sixteen

The Eminence

Our boots trail over the soot staining the large tiles. The silence of the city consumes the castle as well. Our steps echo through the empty halls.

The memory of how angry I was when we first arrived here skims through my mind.

That anger isn't in me anymore. I can't imagine being that angry with any of them now. I love them. I'd do anything for them.

Even die for them ...

The gift of sacrifice.

Am I the sacrifice? Is that what the magic within me is?

My stomach dips, reminding me of the bigger life that I'm now responsible for. A helpless baby unknowingly depends on me.

A heavy sigh falls from my lips.

There's too much responsibility.

The faster this is over the easier it will all be.

My fingers grip my sword and I unsheathe it in a quick movement.

Ryder pulls a sword from his belt as well. He holds it with casual confidence, reminding me of how skilled he is with a weapon.

We're going to get through this. If anyone could win this war, it'd be the four of us.

And if we can't do it ... then the world's fucked.

And it'll no longer be my problem.

"Where should we even be looking?" My whisper crawls up the arching ceilings.

Ryder hesitates for only a moment.

"If it were me, I'd go to the roof. It overlooks the city. You'd be able to see all the way to the coast."

I nod slowly. Without warning, I grip his hand and shudder us away.

He staggers when we land but doesn't fall.

"Okay, you've proved your point. I get it."

I almost smirk at his words.

"Good."

I stalk across the damp concrete. Strong winds pull at my long hair and I curse myself for not tying it back.

"He's not here." Her voice is more of a sob than anything.

I turn toward the small sound of it.

The king's wife stands with her shoulders hunched, her arms wrapped around herself.

Her gaze takes in my appearance as I take in hers. Bruises line her eyes heavily and one is swollen shut. The cut slicing through her lip is puffy and deep.

She's a painful sight to look at. Her once beautiful, glossy hair is knotted around her harsh features.

Ryder shifts at my side.

None of this would have happened if Ryder hadn't wanted a small amount of revenge on his step brother.

He wouldn't have been caught trying to meet this woman, he wouldn't have been imprisoned, and ... I would have never met them.

We all would have lived out simple lives. Simple and easy, but awful lives.

Alone.

I almost want to thank her for sinking her claws into Ryder.

"He's hiding."

Those words catch my attention.

"He's hiding?" Ryder echoes.

"Where?" I take a single step closer to her and she flinches away from me.

Her head turns toward the sea, the wind blows her messy hair back to reveal dark lines around her throat. My attention lingers there on the violent mark against her skin. Pain shoots through my tightly clenched jaw when I force myself to look away.

The sky is a billowing hue of ominous colors behind her.

"There." She points to the few ships lining the coast. "He's waiting for your arrival. He's waiting to destroy you before you even arrive." Three large ships rock against the shore. They're nothing but shadows of details from up here.

A wary feeling tingles down my neck.

What if she's lying?

What if this is all a trap?

But really, what would she have to gain by lying to us? Tristan seems to have caused her more pain than any one person should ever feel in their life.

And yet she stays.

I don't know if she's lying or not.

"I'll come back for you." I take another step closer to her until my boots are skimming against the dirty ends of her long dress. "If you're telling the truth, I'll come back to save you." Her head tips up to me, trying hard to see my features through her swollen eyes. "But if you're lying," my words are spoken carefully and with dark meaning, "just know that I'll still come back for you. But it won't be to *save* you."

"I—I, I'm not lying."

My gaze trails over the fearful tremble of her lower lip.

I walk slowly away from her. When I'm close enough, Ryder slips his hand into mine. It's a reassuring and strong feeling of readiness.

I hold my gaze on the tears that fall from her bloodshot eyes. Her sadness and fear push right into me even after Ryder pulls us away.

We land quietly on one of three ships. In a chance of magic, we land right before the king of Juvar. It's as if we were drawn to him. It's as if Ryder's magic was somehow linked to this man's magic.

And here we stand. Looking up at the one person we've been searching for.

Lucky us.

The sharp angles of his face look down on me with manic interest. A wild look is blazing in his eyes as a smile slashes across his lips.

I had forgotten how terrifying his happiness is.

"Do you know my brother once took something that belonged to me?" Tristan's words are spoken slowly, and with every passing second, I notice that the nix within the waters wade closer to us. A few mortals fight off the nix terrorizing the coast line. Not many, only a dozen, and none of them are winning. The nix slice their talons right through the men, feeding off of the fallen in growing herds.

I nod slowly to Tristan, my grip tightening on the hilt of my sword.

"Do you think it'd be fair for me to take something from him in return?" With speed so fast I don't even see it, he slams his body into mine.

The air is knocked from my lungs. I blink back the stars of pain and slam my sword hard through his abdomen. His body tenses over mine, his weight held above me.

Another wide smile slashes across his face as his magic shakes off of him and through me.

"You're really not nearly as smart as I thought you'd be."

Fury fumes through me and I shudder away from him.

I land on the shore, my boots stomping through the gray foam as I stumble back from the ship. The frames of the ships creak with every passing wave that pushes and pulls against them.

With flashing speed, he stands before me. Nix climb with clawing limbs from the waters. Their quiet cries grow into a building sound of terror. I can't bring myself to look back at the mortals dying behind me.

Tristan looks slowly down at my blade lodged in his side. With a jarring move, he rips it from his flesh. The fire of the city flashes across the clean blade as he studies it.

His pale eyes blaze with power and vengeance and dark magic as he brings his attention back to me.

"I knew you'd bring us our salvation, Miss Storm. I just didn't realize it would be me." He tosses the blade to the rocks and it lands with a clattering sound. Magic like a blazing ember lights his palm. The light grows brighter and brighter with every passing second.

With raw power shaking through his hand, his eyes aglow with rage and annihilation, he's every bit the Eminence Ryder warned me about all that time ago.

And he isn't here to restore our world to the beauty

it once was.

Ryder approaches quietly behind his step brother. Closer and closer he comes.

"I wanted you here for a reason, Miss Storm." Tristan's words are deliberate. As if he's thought about this moment for a long time. "I've recently done a little research on Tomas Storm's only daughter. My mother didn't deserve to die. Especially not by the hands of a piece of fae trash like you." The magic he's holding burns with vengeance, becoming so intense I can feel the power of it in my own chest. His eyes meet mine, his lips pursed into a thin line. "I think it's only fair that you feel how I felt. I want you to feel that feeling of hopelessness." His words drill into me, setting a peculiar frenzy of fear through me. "I know you'll feel that hopelessness when I take Celeste's life."

My lips part, and as my legs lunge toward him, as Ryder's hands fist his brother's shirt, as the nix leap from the sea;

Tristan shudders out of our reach in the blink of an eye.

Chapter Seventeen

Deadly Magic

The thin dragon leather protects my upper body, holding back the sharp attacks of the creatures. But it only covers me so much.

The talons of the nix's claws rip through the flesh of my bare shoulder but I don't feel it. I don't wait for Ryder as I trail after the King of Juvar. I land in the living room of Saint's Inn with the creature still attached to my back. I don't think twice before pulling at its spindly limb. I jerk it to the floor and my flesh tears away beneath its claws. With reckless power and anxious movements, I grab the wine bottle. It shatters against the nix's face as I slam it into its snarling mouth. My muscles are tense and jerking as I quickly slice the edge of the bottle across the creature's neck. Its screams drift off into silence. I storm away from the nix without looking back at it.

"Celeste." I yell her name through the house. My voice carries all through it. Through the glossy windows I spot Daxdyn and Darrio passing out weapons and dragon leathers to our men. I barely even think about the soldiers outside.

"Celeste." My screams are a shrieking cry. My heart

183

pounds harder with every passing second.

Rapid steps pound against the floorboards when I storm up the stairs.

If anything happens, go to the cellar.

I halt in my tracks, remembering what I told her less than twenty-four hours ago.

I take the stairs several at a time. I race to the one place I promised her she'd be safe.

When I swing open the door, I know he's here. Crimson magic glows at the bottom of the stairs. The wood creaks beneath my steps as I stalk closer to him. The color of his magic is the only light. It fumes over his features in dark shadows and eerie blood red colors.

His palm is held tightly over my aunt's mouth. No tears stream down her beautiful face. She looks furious as he holds her tightly to his chest.

She's never been intimidated by men.

Not even by the Eminence, apparently.

"She made a good show of running from me. You'd have been so proud."

Another creaking step brings me just a few feet from him.

"Release her and you can have me."

Laughter shakes through him, curving the angles of his face into a look of terrifying happiness.

"I don't know how many times I can say this; *I don't want you* anymore, Miss Storm." The light in his hand blazes into so much power it makes my breath catch in my lungs. "All I want now is to watch you suffer. I'm going to take everything you love and I'm going to destroy it. And then, I'm going to rule over the seven realms. I'm going to rule over your entire life. And I want you to see what we could have been together."

The fire magic within me stings through my palms as I try to find the best way to harm him without burning my aunt and this whole fucking house to the ground.

"But for right now," his hand rises and I leap for him. The crimson magic slams hard into her chest. "I want you to suffer."

I slam into him but my eyes are held on Celeste as she slumps to the floor. The crimson color glows through her body, emanating from her chest until it fumes all through her shoulders and legs. It consumes her entirely.

A quiet sound of pain leaves her lips on an empty breath. Her eyes hold mine and I know the moment the life leaves her body. A glossy look fills her gaze and the crimson color drains from her.

My palms are against her unseen wound. I shove at the magic within me, trying to find the healing powers that I know every fae possesses.

Warm energy shakes through me. I feel it. I know it's what I need. I know it's the magic that could save her.

But it doesn't.

The bright white magic that pushes from my palms simply dissolves into her slacken body.

I release it, but it never absorbs.

She's gone. Several moments pass like that. When I jerk my hands away, a charred and decaying texture starts to burn across her body, leaving a corpse behind.

A startling breath rips from my lungs. Moisture burns my eyes as I stare at her.

Darrio and Dax's voice sound far off in my thoughts as they enter the house above us.

"The nix should be tearing up the coast by now. I really should greet them properly." Tristan's words are an empty sound within my mind.

Pain strikes through my chest, pushing sorrow all through me.

But another feeling is stronger.

Rage shakes through me and as he walks past me, I

grip his slender leg. I jerk hard until his palms hit the gritty floor. With fuming anger and burning magic, I jump on him. My knees hit the floor and I waste no time slamming his head into the concrete. Power like I've never felt tears through me. As I slam his head to the floor for the second time, fire blazes from my palms. It strikes across his jaw and up his face. The smell of burning flesh fills the small cellar and I can't seem to stop the fire from pouring from my veins.

His shrieks echo around the room until they stop abruptly.

In the blink of an eye, he's gone. He's shuddered away from me once again.

The fire halts in an instant and I waste no time storming up the stairs. I push past Darrio and Daxdyn. My feet are stomping across the dirt outside as quickly as my legs will carry me.

Nefarious breathes out a happy puff of air. I stroke his scales without thought. It's as if I'm having a silent pep talk with the creature. His silver eyes shine my reflection back at me. My hair is a tangled mess. Ash and blood stain my face.

But I don't see any of it.

All I see are her empty eyes staring back at me in my mind.

I feel Daxdyn behind me. I feel his tension and apprehension and anger all rolled up into a suffocating ball of energy.

"I want you two to take Nefarious to the shore. Our men are already there." Probably fighting a losing battle. I keep that awful thought to myself. "I want you guys to guide him across the sea and have him torch those fucking creatures before they even make it to the coast."

"That's a one person job. Dax can manage. Let me help you." Darrio's reasonable statement sets me further on edge.

He dies saving you.

I can't stand the thought of another person dying because of me.

It isn't fair.

"No." And without another word, I shudder away from them.

The coast is in chaos. Blood and bodies litter the ground. Nix slash through mortals. Their talons tear right through them. The fae aren't much better. Their magic lights up the darkness, striking through it with bloody power. I catch a glimpse of Ryder as he shudders in, surprising a group of nix right before he slices through them with my very own sword.

A warm feeling flutters through me as I realize he didn't let me leave the weapon behind in Juvar. It's a short-lived feeling of affection.

Streven shudders in at my side just in time to clench a nix by its throat. The creature's talons reach out for my face, whipping past my nose by mere centimeters.

Streven slams the creature to the ground and uses the heel of his boot to silence its cries. I turn my head toward him, and for a second, I consider thanking him.

And then I realize he'll never make my aunt smile again. I liked him for making her smile. Her smile's gone and neither of us will ever see it again.

His brows lower with a look of confusion as he stares at my empty expression.

My throat tightens and I force myself to step past him.

I push the thoughts from my mind as my gaze searches the shore for a man with too much power and not enough face.

I hope it scars him. I hope he's charred from my magic for the rest of his short life.

Heat rains down from the heavens. I look up as a roaring sound of anger fills the air.

A prideful feeling consumes me as Darrio and

Daxdyn lead Nefarious over the shore.

The dominant sound of the dragon horse's war cry echoes across the waters, making the animal fiercer and more demanding to look at. Most of the nix shrink back from it, scurrying away from the battle on the land to slip back into the safety of the water.

The dragon horse's wide wings sweep over the sea, beating down on it as it breathes flames over the limbs of the nix trying to crawl out of the waters.

Our soldiers stand waiting for the nix to flee the wrath of the longma. As I train my flames on the nix before me, other soldiers slice and rip apart the creatures climbing up the shore.

We're winning.

I think.

Is this what winning feels like?

Razor sharp talons sink into my calf. Wild flames are burning across the nix's arm and still the thing tries to attack me.

I kick my boot into its arm, detaching the creature from my leg. The shores are ablaze, flames move with every nix that tries to escape the sea only to be demolished by the fae waiting.

I'm pleased with our work. We're doing well.

Perhaps I was worried for nothing.

And that feeling of achievement washes away as his fingers grip my throat.

Just as I had hoped, black ash is scraping over one side of his sneering face. The flesh isn't fully there. Black char and slick burns make up half his features now.

My fingers dig into his arm but he only tightens his hold on me.

"I wanted you to suffer. That was before I realized how annoyingly resilient you are. Now I want you dead."

You think a burned face is bad? There are far worse things.

I gasp for a breath. His smile falters for an instant as I grip his dick hard enough to make him wince.

Fire burns through my veins. I release it with shaking power.

My flames are barely ignited when a high pitched cry leaves him and he stumbles back from me, clutching his tiny dick like there was even much there to roast.

I stalk closer to him. His jaw tightens as he straightens.

His palm rises and once again, I feel that combusting power of his shake through my chest. The energy burns brightly in his hands. Cautiously, I step back from him, wary of the quick magic I know he's bound to use on me.

I reach within myself for the power Loki taught me. I can't help but realize the god did in fact give me a gift.

My fingers arch painfully and I try with force to bring his hand down.

But he's stronger.

The magic in his hand burns bright and unwavering.

Fire flashes from my palms but Tristan sidesteps it. He shudders away just in time only to flicker back right in front of me. The hard angle of his head slams against mine. The force of it washes spots of bright white all through my vision. His fingers grip my wrist tightly, averting my flames to the damp ground as he holds his powerful magic in the other hand.

He's poised, prepared to end me once and for all.

Nefarious' rumbling roar signals his arrival and my stomach sinks from the sound of it.

"No." My voice is a shrieking sound filled with fear and heartache and a knowing sense of what's to come.

Darrio stands between the wings of the dragon horse. He's tall with determination etched upon his handsome face. He's ready to leap, ready to save me from my stupid, stupid decisions.

It all happens so quickly.

Nefarious is just above Tristan and he turns at the sound of the longma's roar. The magic in Tristan's hand is released the moment he sees Darrio crouching for an attack.

May you have the strength to understand what you can and cannot change.

The Traveler's voice echoes through my mind but I know this is something I cannot change. I'm not fast enough. Tristan is too quick. His magic is too powerful.

And there's only one way this will end.

At the last moment, Daxdyn shoves his brother, pushing him from Nefarious and letting him hit the ground without caution. The magic in Tristan's hand releases. It burns so brightly I can't help but memorize the crimson colors that wash over Daxdyn's beautiful and innocent face.

Just before it hits him firmly in the chest.

Chapter Eighteen

The Sacrifice

The crimson magic bursts through Daxdyn with so much force he falls from the dragon horse. His eyes hold mine as he lands along the shore, the water lapping against his dirty boots. Terror pushes through me as I watch the magic burst through him. The magic begins to consume him slowly.

A heavy, sobbing breath shakes though my lungs and I turn my gaze to the dangerous man in front of me. Tristan's gaze settles on me with a pleased look on his disgusting little face.

Power radiates all through me. It's a foreign feeling and I latch on to it. It's strong. Too strong. It's consuming and raw and deadly. It doesn't belong to me, but I hold onto it. I keep the feeling of it within me, memorizing the toxic energy until it's mine to keep.

Even if it is the power of the Eminence and I am just an ordinary fae with an unordinary gift of mimicking magic.

My hands shake as the power caresses my body, threatening to devour me from the inside out. I take a stalking step closer to Tristan and his eyes narrow suspiciously on me.

He has the nerve to reach out and grip my jaw in his thin hands. He tilts my head back and forth in his palm.

"I never want to forget the woman who brought me all my glory." The burnt edge of his lips tips up in a smile.

Energy pools through me in drowning waves.

His lips part and just before he can say another fucking thing, I shove my palm against his chest so hard he stumbles back from me.

The crimson color ignites within his core. A mimicking form of his own magic eats him alive. He stares down at it in astonishment. It highlights the sharp angles of his features. I step closer and closer to him, my eyes locked on that magic that's burning up inside him.

He crumbles to the ground, his knees hitting with a solid thud.

Finally, he looks up at me. The blood red color creeps up his face.

I lower myself until I can look him dead in the eye.

"Never forget the woman who brought you all your glory," I whisper.

The magic eats through him at a quicker pace than

it did my aunt. It's as if his energy was already dark and the magic absorbed right into that darkness at an alarming rate.

When his body hits the ground, it's nothing more than a charred corpse.

But I don't wait to see his death.

I rush to Daxdyn.

Ryder holds my blade in his hand. It's pointed to the ground. The war is all but forgotten. His lips are parted and he does nothing but stare in astonishment at his friend lying lifelessly on the ground.

My body lowers over Daxdyn's, and I find that oddly, he isn't decaying. My hand skims over the smooth leather covering his chest. He's fine. He's still as perfect as ever.

Except he's not.

He's not *alive*. Not even dragon's leather could protect him from the power of the Eminence.

Every simple act of love he's ever shown me swarms through my mind and heart. Tears of anger and tears of pain slip down my cheeks as I stare silently at his peaceful face. The smooth curve of his lips isn't tilted into a smile for once.

I couldn't save him. The least aggressive man I've

ever met, and the sweetest man I've ever loved, has left me.

Feelings flood my chest, tightening my throat until I can't manage a simple breath.

There's still warmth in his palm and I cling to it like it's the last thing I'll ever have to keep of him. My thumbs worry back and forth against his knuckles as if I can comfort him even after he's already gone.

Some people believe there's a comfort in death. A comfort in knowing there's no more suffering.

Only beauty.

For some selfish reason I can't find comfort in knowing this beautiful man is no longer mine to hold.

A sob shakes through my chest and Darrio's big hand slowly brushes up and down my spine.

My fingertips tremble as I push over Daxdyn's chest, feeling the silence of his heart against my palm. My wet tears kiss his cheek as I lean closer. The first real memory I have of Daxdyn threatens to break the last little ounce of strength I have left.

He gave me life when I thought mine was already gone. When I thought I was dying, he held me. He pressed his gentle lips to my forehead and he held me like he'd never let me go.

An unsteady breath fills my lungs and I lean into him. My lips brush against his temple slowly. My eyes clench tightly closed, and for an instant, I pretend he's still mine to keep. I pretend his playful laughter still fills my aching heart. I pretend his strong arms still surround me. I pretend he'll grow old with me. With Darrio and Ryder. And with all the beautiful children he'll never get to see.

For just a moment, I pretend his heart still beats for me.

Fury like I've never felt burns through my veins at the injustice of it all. Anger starts to overtake the sorrow flooding my chest.

This was my sacrifice?

It isn't fair. There's too much terribleness in the world for me to live without his calming energy filling my chest.

The gods blessed me more than any other.

But I don't want it.

I want him.

Reckless power shakes my hands and my fingers fist his shirt. The smooth dragons leather wrinkles beneath my touch, until I can't control the magic any more.

Bright, white light slams through my palms, forcing

its way out from the depths of my pain. It trembles from me and into him. It makes the earth beneath us quiver, altering it just slightly. The blinding color surrounds him and me, haloing us until the rest of the world dissolves away. The nix disappear from our lands. The fires disperse. The dark skies fade away into warming colors of gold and white and bright blue skies.

I don't know what the magic is, but it feels right. It's pure and calming.

Just like Daxdyn Riles.

So, I usher it out in waves, helping it along until I'm weak and using his body to support my own. My wings expand of their own accord as if the magic demands them to release themselves. I feel it start to tear away at me. First at my beautiful feathers; pulling at them. Ebony colors swirl around us, inking through the white magic as my feathers twirl in the breeze. A weight falls from my body. The moment my wings fall away, I feel it. Not just in my shoulders but deep within me.

The magic strips me until I'm nothing more than a broken woman clinging to a broken man.

Nearly every ounce of the powerful energy pours from me until I'm lying over him like a worthless shield. I give him everything I have.

Peaceful sounds of the ocean return, lapping in and

attempting to coax my exhausted emotions into a dull and empty feeling.

Warm fingertips skim up my side, threatening the numbness.

"Kara, you're crushing me."

Dax's voice comes out in a rasping whisper. The small sound of it thunders right through my heart, I swear it.

My arms cling to him tighter as my eyes fling open and the most beautiful starry-gray gaze meets mine. Humor and life and love shines within them.

A trembling breath shakes through me just before I slam my lips against his.

His strong arms hold me to his hard body, but my fingertips refuse to pull away from the steady pounding of his heart.

A quietness fills my veins where a hum of energy once burned.

Quiet magic tingles within me. My all-powerful magic is gone.

But he's still here; right where he should be.

Daxdyn wasn't the sacrifice the gods anticipated.

I was.

Hopeless Sacrifice

Chapter Nineteen

Several Quiet Months Later

My whole life has been about survival.

Just making it through the day, finding meaning in the loneliness.

It's so different now that my chest physically aches to think about it.

I survived. I survived not only the war, but my life.

I survived myself.

I'll never admit it, but they saved me. These three arrogant fae saved me when I didn't even realize I needed them to.

Let's not give them all the glory, though. I did all the grunt work, after all.

Nefarious' hot breath sweeps over my palm as he steals another burnt crisp of meat from my hand. I stand on the porch while he leans into it to be closer to me and his crispy treats. I trail my fingers over the dark scales of his snout. A humming sound of approval shakes through him.

He turned out to be a good little house pet. Even if the men won't actually let me move him into the house. My favorite dragon horse has to sleep outside. Poor little guy.

The sunset casts an orange but beautiful color across the dusty streets. The small white flowers I planted at the base of the porch sway in the cool breeze.

It's a perfect day. Clear blue skies and fluffy white clouds look down on our little lives.

A warm palm pushes slowly over the curve of my growing belly. I know who it is as his body settles against mine, wrapping me safely in his arms.

"You know, my sisters swear there are twins in here." Daxdyn's lips press to the curve of my neck.

A smile pushes across my lips as I lean into his strong body.

"Hmmm, I think your sisters are full of shit. I'll be lucky if I survive one arrogant fae baby, don't even mention two."

The boards creek as someone strides out to us. Darrio saunters over, his palms pushing low down my stomach.

"It could be three. There could be three little arrogant fae babies in there." His small smile makes my heart melt.

Their happiness almost makes me unafraid of what it'll be like soon.

I know the baby will be taken care of because of these three men.

Just like me.

When things quieted in the world, people realized Ryder was their king. He was King Ryder. For all of one royal day. Before he corrected them. I love that he doesn't want that title. I love that he'd rather the humans have a leader who's lived and understands the mortal realm more than he does.

Or maybe he wants a quiet life just like I do.

A palace is not where our future lies. Our past, our present, and future are right here.

At Saints Inn: former most prestigious whore house in all the land.

Soon little pitter patter feet will fill this house the way moans and cheap sex used to. Lady Ivory would be shocked.

Actually, I know she'd be amazed by it. She'd love that the house that my father built her was filled with love and life.

It's everything she always wanted for me.

It's all I ever wanted for myself.

It still feels too quiet without her. I miss her. I miss her advice and I miss the comfort that her simple presence provided.

She's gone but I still feel her all around me. Her memory is everywhere in this house.

Her memory is within me. And it always will be.

Ryder pulls at my arm until I face the three of them. Nefarious huffs a jealous sigh before lowering himself down to lie on the ground. Ryder leans his temple against mine as his big palm rests against my navel.

"Fuck, let's just hope they're not anything like their mother, or none of us will make it."

Gentle magic swarms me and I use it to my advantage. I touch my finger to the tip of his nose and it sparks on contact. It isn't much. It isn't raw and powerful like it once was. And I don't want it to be. I like my quiet Hopeless fae magic. I like that I can still use it to piss them off whenever I want.

Ryder curses from the stinging feel of my magic and their rumbling laughter skims through me.

I'm surrounded.

I'm completely surrounded by asshole fae men.

And I'd never want it any other way.

Epilogue

Darrio
Two Years Later

The small boy who lies in my lap shares a smile so similar to his mother's. But damn if those stormy eyes aren't all mine.

He's going to break hearts. We can only hope he has better people skills than Daxdyn.

Or me I suppose.

Kara looks at me from beneath long lashes as I read The Tale of Walton Whitetail for the hundred and eighth time tonight. Kara always insists that I read. She says the kids like my voice.

I think Kara likes my voice. But I'd read this fucking book a million times if it made her happy.

A prideful look is in her gaze as she watches our baby boy fall asleep in my arms.

A deep, warm feeling of love blankets over me as I hold Tomas a little closer. His dark lashes flutter as he starts to doze.

Finally.

Finally, the little demon is asleep.

He's an angel of course. But he's also a little shit just like his mother sometimes.

I lower my tone, preparing to read the last page for the last time tonight.

Kara catches my attention as I babble on about foxholes and rabbit holes and … her fingers unsnap her jeans as she holds my gaze.

And the fucking end. Good night, Walton Whitetail. Until we meet again. Tomorrow. And the next night and the next.

As deathly quiet as I possibly can, I slip from the tiny bed. It groans in protest but thank the gods, he stays asleep.

My heart flutters as small snores follow me even after I close the child's door.

Kara's arms wrap around me the moment I'm close enough and I sink into her small frame. My lips press against hers slowly, tasting every part of this beautiful woman.

She has this amazing ability to push away everything

else until it's just us.

Until it's not.

"Mmm, you still have to help Dax and Ryder." At the sound of her words, my palms halt against her smooth abdomen.

"Dax and Ryder?"

My tongue strokes along hers until she moans into me. Her lips tip up in a smirk against my mouth and I try my best to kiss away her words.

But she doesn't allow it.

"Ryder and Dax are still reading to Celeste downstairs."

Celeste. Tomas is the easy one. They're similar in appearance, but one is a little darling and one is a little asshole.

Just like her father.

"I think we have a few minutes to spare," I whisper against her mouth before raking my teeth across her bottom lip.

Her sparkling eyes narrow on me but a hint of a smile pulls at her mouth. I've always been able to do that to her; piss her off and make her crazy all at the same time.

Her small hand tugs at mine while we make our way downstairs.

"That's right, then the gorgeous princess let down her long hair and not one, but three glorious knights rescued her from the towering tower." Dax's overly enthusiastic voice carries through the dark living room.

He's a great dad. Just like I knew he'd be. Kara thinks Dax helps me. He makes me a better father.

He does more than she'll ever know though. He makes me a better person.

Just like she does.

"Did *they* really rescue *her* though if she had to help them up the tower?" Kara folds her arms across her chest and my brother smirks at her from over his shoulder. "She probably could have rescued herself."

Ryder stands from the couch, stretching his arms high above his head.

"The princess definitely could have just rescued herself. But not everyone's as self-reliant as you are, beautiful." Ryder winks at her and she rolls her eyes at him.

Dax stands slowly and a small girl who looks so much like him is asleep in his arms. Dark hair fans across Celeste's angelic face.

She's so much sweeter when she's asleep.

Kara presses her lips to Celeste's forehead, pushing back the child's unruly hair as she goes. The three of us trail behind Dax. Every small creak of the stairs makes my heart stop.

I just want sleep. Being a father is amazing. But no one tells you that you'll never sleep again.

Like terrified ninjas, we take her to their bedroom. A dim light shines against the floor of the tiny room. A nightlight to keep away the monsters as Kara likes to say. I don't know why. Kara would fucking destroy any monster that ever threatened their lives. She doesn't take my shit, she's certainly not going to give monsters a fighting chance.

Dax tucks Celeste into the bed that sits right next to her brother's.

Celeste turns in her sleep until she's facing Tomas, their small hands just inches apart.

I can't help but feel my heart storm to life every time I look at them.

Kara leans her head back into my chest and I waste no time wrapping my arms around her. She calms me when I don't even realize I need it.

Before we met, I never realized I was missing a

beautiful train wreck like Zakara Storm.

Sometimes it seems surreal.

I don't deserve any of it.

I never expected in all of my long and lonely existence to have beautiful children. Or a beautiful family.

Or a beautiful life.

The Hopeless End

Also by A.K. Koonce

The Mortals and Mystics Series

Fate of the Hybrid, Prequel

When Fate Aligns, Book one

When Fate Unravels, Book two

When Fate Prevails, Book three

The Resurrection Series
Resurrection Island, Book one

The Royal Harem Series
The Hundred Year Curse
The Curse of the Sea
The Legend of the Cursed Princess

About A.K. Koonce

A.K. Koonce is a USA Today bestselling author. She's a mom by day and a fantasy and paranormal romance writer by night. She keeps her fantastical stories in her mind on an endless loop while she tries her best to focus on her actual life and not that of the spectacular, but demanding, fictional characters who always fill her thoughts.

Made in the USA
Columbia, SC
21 September 2024

42600895R00133